An Indifferent Sun

Copyright © 2024 Lot Kiely

All rights reserved.
No part of this publication may be reproduced, stored or transmitted in any form or by any means, electronic, mechanical, photocopying, recording, or otherwise, without written permission from the author.

This book is a work of fiction. All names, characters, places, and incidents are the product of the author's imagination or are used fictitiously. Any resemblance to actual persons, living or dead, events, or locales is entirely coincidental.

Lot Kiely

An Indifferent Sun
An Fuarthé Ghrian

LONG BEAR

Prologue
The End

 The Sun is white. That is my strongest memory of the world. In the absence of a present, I am haunted by memories. I feel them in the lining of my abdomen, weighing me down. The feeling of unease, as if I am being followed by a black dark hole of despair, is my constant company. Blinded perception can be a desperate thing, but how horrible it is to be aware of one's own.

 When I was young, so long ago, I thought I knew my place in the delicate stacks of hierarchies. They all came crumbling down when I watched them come one by one. Their fervor was palpable. Each one rushed through the tight corridor. I watched as, in their panic, they did not perceive the ever narrowing of the walls around them. First, the few in front slowed. I could see them faltering behind like an arrangement of dominos sequencing. Then the consternation spread like wildfire. The hysteria became a bubbling stampede, halted in the tragic predicament. Their hands grasped out from the trapped mass, desperate to be free. Blood began pooling as those near the walls were crushed against the sharp walls. I knew they would only keep coming and their tortuous fate was doomed to the slow suffocation as the ones before them. That was long ago.

And now the horror of anticipation consumes my every waking hour. I crawl along through worries which I cannot confide.

I have become a creature of the darkness, a creature from the deepest of oceans floors. The memories of how others had perceived me follow me most of all. The melody of acceptance, the sunbeam of an honest welcome were as alien to me as the breathless air that I find surrounding me now. My only song is the lament of my own existence. I see their faces looking upon me and I know the revolt they sensed from the very soul behind my eyes. What I am, they seemed to sense so purely.

I find it difficult to reflect in chronological order, but I will try. Memories within memories are not easy to produce when the strain of emotion runs through everything. It is like dark shadows spilling out from every open window. But again, I will try, as the last one of our kind.

Part 1

1

The Beginning
9/23/2499 11:45AM

In the humid midday Sun, Rhode steps across the busy pedestrian crossing. The compressed nature of the port city of Ji adds to the oppressive and thick atmosphere.

"Sulsu, hello!" Rhode quickens her step. "Su! *Hi!*" She feels confused. *Didn't she hear me? She is looking right at me.* As Rhode approaches the storefront, a man exits the main door. A little bell overhead makes a gentle click and a lingering vibration. Rhode smiles as she steps out of the man's way and is greeted with a sour accusatory face which nearly causes her to jump back. She feels her olive cheeks blush. In an instant, she realizes her error. The man wears a blue headdress and formal attire. Sulsu, a girl who Rhode instantly recognised from the Ves neighborhood, stands outside the storefront in a turquoise veil and a simple matching dress. Above them, a bright screen gleams with a fast paced news program. A vivid blue ribbon moves across the bottom of the screen with developing updates and continuous references to the Light Ceremony.

Of the many festivals in Great Sular, the Time of Light was the largest and most observed. A day of piety, or religious prayer for those of the Thrinaic faith, loud greetings and happy, jubilant greetings are fully disapproved of. *How disrespectful of me!* Rhode bowed her head and mouthed an apology. Turning now to Sulsu, who appears somewhat startled, Rhode quietly says, "Hello. I am sorry for having shouted. I forgot about the day." It had been a long time since Rhode had observed such practices herself. Cymt, the country across Niivrheon Bay, sits under a vast sheet of ice. The towns and cities are situated along the western border of a protruding mass. It had been Rhode's home for the past six years, since the Mass Relegation. Rhode's bulky brown dress and cloak, which marked her as a visitor to this land, now seems more conspicuous against the ceremonial colors.

"I didn't know you were back in town," Sulsu says.

"I wasn't sure you recognised me."

"Oh, I recognised you. Although you look different." Sulsu's gaze moves up Rhode's body. "But that is living in Cymt, I suppose." As Sulsu brushes her hand to her face, pulling back her lace veil, Rhode sees her raise her left eyebrow. "Are you leaving today?" Sulsu motions to the bulky suitcase hanging hard from Rhode's shoulder. Rhode unconsciously shifts the suitcase in front of her abdomen.

"No," Rhode says, forcing a smile. "Well, I am. My boat only arrived in Ji yesterday. I am on my way now to take a train to Hant." She points to the metal stairway at the end of the block which leads to the station. "I have family to visit before I go. My boat leaves for Cymt again in four more days." Rhode tries to hide the bitterness of those words. Rhode was among the group of children from Great Sular who were sent to Cymt to boost their declining population. The Elders of Great Sular had envisioned the Mass Relegation would pacify the Cymtian authorities. It had been announced as the ultimate answer to the growing tension between the principal nations. Now fifteen years old, Rhode is finally permitted to visit Great Sular annually.

Sulsu looks confused. "I didn't realize you could visit for so long. We must make plans to see one another *next* time you are here." Sulsu speaks in a slow and insincere manner that leaves Rhode feeling flustered. Before Rhode can think of anything else to say, her thoughts are interrupted by the sound of the approaching steam train.

"My train! I must go," *I will be late. I was late to begin with.* There is a high pitched hum from the above screen as the coverage changes to a well dressed man and woman being interviewed on a long concrete couch. The woman sits effortlessly straight with her long pale legs crossed casually, while the man has his head resting against his elbow. The words at the bottom of the screen read Kidra Pi Tel and Dant Pi Tel.

"To Hant, is it? You must get a look at the Pi Tels while you're there," Sulsu continues to speak in her quiet tone even as Rhode rushes down the block. "Those two are still larger than life!"

Rhode runs awkwardly, her large suitcase now clutched within her arms. The stairway is further than it looked. She pushes her right hand into the opening of her zipped suitcase. *Still there.*

She thinks back to the sight of the orthodox dress. How could she have forgotten? The festival today is only the beginning of the great celebration to mark the introduction of the Thrinaic faith all those years ago, following the Time of The Sun. This world had been all but destroyed; Mankind would have vanished completely without the Thrinaic founder Trem Psy. Rhode had not factored this festival into her decision to visit at this time. Rather, she seized the opportunity to leave Cymt with both hands, hard and frenzied. Her days living in Cymt had been long. The icey blanket that sits over the perilous country was the least of her concerns.

She coughs as she approaches the great black train. The yellow steam nearly obstructs her vision as she has to push past the non passengers who stand outside the open train doors. She shudders as she feels one of their tugging fingers against her woolen cloak. Those sickening myrlorx are more plentiful in this region now and Rhode is unnerved by the changes to their appearance. They had always been small in numbers and certainly were not counted towards the general population of Great Sular. They were known to venture into cities to beg for food and, in recent years, Rhode had seen on news reports, have taken to wearing thick masks of a childlike appearance.

As she moves slowly through the aisle, she thinks back to what Sulsu had said. *What was it? The Pi Tels?* Local celebrities have been commonplace in this region for as long as Rhode could remember. She had nearly forgotten these odd customs. Often hand picked by the elders themselves, the celebrated members of the elite circle are beloved by the masses. The difference to where she lives now is striking. Cymt is old and dark, made of ice that never melts and people who never release themselves to benign joys. She forces herself to look out the window, eager to let her thoughts drift away from what may await her when she should return. The locals there have a saying, "Pidwix a duauch ycudum yus not oddit, 'ul heron duom I fleswull 'n 'tan." *Don't waste your dying wish on the heat of the Sun, for a heart of ice will never melt.*

2
The Celebrated
9/23/2499 4:17PM

Dant sits on a bed, his hand running through his thinning black hair. Kidra stands beside the bed with her champagne pink empire gown waving gracefully as her foot taps beneath it. "Well, what do you suggest?" She asks, eyes wide, and stare fixed forward.

"I'm thinking, aren't I?" Dant sinks further into the elegant sheets, letting his head touch the ornately carved wooden headboard. Kidra turns quickly. Her loud perm evokes the essence of hundreds of years past.

"We need to do *something*," she utters almost inaudibly as a shudder moves down her body. She looks back to the closet. To that double door walk-in closet she had heard so much about during the hologrammed invitation. Jua and Ash La Kes had been just dying to show them the new house. A pre-ceremony lohqra and a house tour with several other couples in high standing was an acceptable side step in their social climbing, so Kidra had agreed. She moves a chair to the closet and tucks the top rail underneath the brass door knob.

"Oh, well done, Kidra, that'll do it," Dant comments sarcastically. "All eyes are on us. Well, they will be downstairs and they will be out there!"

"Don't you dare speak to me like that!" Kidra's voice trembles. She can feel her heart pounding through her chest.

"We need to get out of here. We need to go."

"If we leave him, what do you think they'll do to him?"

"It's inevitable."

Kidra hesitates and wraps her arms around herself.

Continuing with wavering conviction, Dant whispers "We can't be here when he is found. We'll be…" As Dant moves to straighten himself, a sudden thud comes from the closet. In a flash, he recalls the events of the last several decades and feels a surge of the shadow of calamity that had been stalking him.

Dant and Kidra had considered themselves in high social standing within the central Thrinaic sect. They had the envy of their friends when their marriage began. Both the eldest children of oracles, they had sat front and center to all the festive activities; For years they were the first to be given the blessing of light. All his life, he *knew* this meant something important. As he grew older he found less and less comfort in this fact and now it seems like nothing at all. He has vaguely feared their peers felt the same way, despite his efforts to advance his political career. Two weeks ago, Ash La Kes had approached him in the market, bragging about her new home, the reap of which followed her recent wedding to Jua. Ash's long black hair and large eyes hadn't changed since she was a girl. In his youth, Dant had seen admiration, almost longing, in her gaze at him. In recent years, he saw in her eyes only that hollow routine tact that was the throughline of all his interactions now. He is not the special young heir that he once was and he sees that as clearly in the eyes of others as in his own reflection. Despite this, invitations and praises continue. Dant wonders if this will carry on out of habit or if the favor will gradually shift elsewhere.

    Dant had wanted to ignore the invitation however he knew Kidra was desperate to keep their social standing up, even if it had to be artificially propped up with falsitudes and exaggerated bluffs. Dant never learnt how to socially navigate this world without relying on his status, and in his youth, but for Cagh, he would be inclined to disappear from it completely. And Kidra spurred him on. She was the one who had wanted a child. She had persuaded the elders to select a suitable child for their care. The ceremony was grand. Dant remembers the light shining from the moon and bouncing off the blue of the magnificent crowd. Then they settled into as normal of a life as ever they could. The child grew quickly and grew taller than most. Tall and silent. Bringing Ghli tonight had not been his decision and Kidra, although she had not admitted it, would have also preferred to keep him at a distance from such events. Another soiree would certainly be full of unconscious traps to catch him out. The subtle changes that they had seen in Ghli were cumulative to their great fear. Fear for themselves and for the Thrinaic faith itself.

The closet doors open in a slow creak. The chair becomes off balance and gravity pulls it to the floor. "Explain to him, Dant. Explain that everyone will be looking for him exactly; *him*."

3
The Train
9/23/2499 4:32PM

Rhode lets out a sigh. The journey has slowed since the train left Ji Station. Lying on the lowest bed of the stacked compartments, she allows her right leg to fall to the aisle. The rips in the fabric on the canvas beneath her are of no help to her increasing discomfort. The train has been moving for hours now, slowing when approaching a new city and then speeding rapidly against the increasingly domesticated trees. The smog has become a constant. *Unreal how gray this country is.* With every city stop, Rhode had seen more of the poor grasping myrlorx with their dirt studded hands and their infant masks. But for those masks, she would have vomited at their sight. Rhode shudders again at the thought of their fingers touching her cloak and has a fleeting thought of burning it.

"Keep the aisles clear." A loud monotone voice startles her. The train employee continues walking down the aisle without looking back. The central screen that runs across the ceiling of the train flashes another sign on train etiquette. Rhode retrieves her suitcase from the hanging cage beneath her seat. She almost hugs it as she places her hand carefully between the teeth of the open zipper.

"Soon, Nal," she whispers softly. Letting her gaze settle to the window again, she can see a tall slanted tower approaching in the distance, marking the city of Hant. Its silver and magenta stripes are striking against the gray sky above and the bright sunset revealing its lower edges. Rhode can hardly believe it is so far away considering its immense size already. She removes her glowing scroll carefully from her bag and unrolls the horizontal screen. It doesn't take her long to find another news report on the Pi Tels and their role in the upcoming Light Ceremony. Rhode bites down on her thin lower lip as the memories flood back to her.

Rhode is thrust forward as the train slows suddenly and halts. She lets out a gasp, momentarily winded. Through the window she sees only wispy trees blowing against the crimson horizon. Above her, the central linear screen now flickers a faint red. She becomes aware of how crowded the train is as disgruntled vocalizations are uttered around her. Breathing out, she holds her suitcase against her chest. In her peripheral vision, she sees a shadow move across the train window. As she turns, she jumps slightly and instinctively moves to the aisle of the train. In the bottom corner of the window, a long thin hand is gently pressed against the glass. A silicone face with large round eyes and bright red cheeks raises itself slowly and peers through at Rhode. She steps backwards and nearly falls onto a man rising from his bed. She looks back at him apologetically only to see his eyes glaring fiercely to the window to his right. Following his gaze, Rhode tenses. Four more sets of those false blue shiny eyes are pressed against the windows.

The mounting tension in the train releases. Rhode hears an angry shout behind her. In the front of the train is a heavy bang as another passenger ragefully hits his fist into the adjoining car door. Passengers start to move; Some move to the windows to hit at the glass where the myrlorx stand and some push their way to the doors of the vehicle. Rhode looks back and forth, willing herself to make a plan. There are no announcements, no hint of what has happened. A crack in the window lets out a continuous creak as it grows larger. Rhode feels herself walking backwards over the aisle. She stops as she meets resistance. As she turns her head, she feels her knees buckle and she collapses to the floor. Behind her is a myrlorx, standing tall and crooked underneath a stained yellow cloak. Its mask grins at her with red cupid lips. Looking up from the floor, Rhode sees a twitch on the jaw hiding beneath the pale pink silicone. Rhode is nearly trampled as the myrlorx passes her. The creaking from the window turns into a shatter of glass. Gasps escape around her. Myrlorx are crawling into the train from the windows in front and the doors behind. Rhode becomes aware of a strong odor filling the small car. She holds her heavy suitcase to her chest with one arm as she awkwardly crawls forward, allowing herself to become bruised and bashed under wet and bare feet. She feels a hard pull on her cloak and she hastily loosens it from her neck. She can see more and more myrlorx climbing through the doors of the train. Hearing a hard scream behind her, she throws herself through the group of myrlorx and off of the train, landing on her back and still clutching her unzipped bag. Another masked face stares at her from above and reaches its boney fingers towards her. Suddenly, it pulls away, as if taken aback.

Rhode looks down to see Nal on her chest, growling. Nal's body appears small due to her young age, but her central horn is remarkably thick. Solceros are nearly extinct; Now bred only in Cymt, Rhode does not doubt this is an unusual sight, even to the wild myrlorx standing over her. Rhode grasps Nal in her hands, frightened she would run off. Abandoning her bag, Rhode runs with Nal towards a soft light visible through the naked trees. She sees other passengers who had escaped running in the same direction.

Behind her, the myrlorx remain on the train. Muted shrieks begin to quiet.

Nal begins to shake in Rhode's arms. "I'm sorry, baby." She can hardly feel her arms anymore with Nal's weight. She slows into a hasted walk through the trees, feeling the eyes of other passengers watching her as the glow of the approaching small town grows. She maneuvers Nal under one arm and uses the other gently to stroke her tuft of long brown fur on top of her humped back. Nal's small eyes close.

After walking for what seems like an hour, Rhode feels the soft earth underneath her turn to concrete and she starts to get her bearings out of the woods. A street light above flickers, though appears dim compared to the theatrical display of fire moving through the street. Blue-robed men march slowly around the fire, chanting gently.

"The light, the light. The future is light."

4
Teven
9/23/2499 5:28PM

The lighting is warm and festive. The flat light of the imitation fireplace intensifies against the decrepit gray bricks that suspend the wooden boards. People, young and old, jovial and lethargic, push their way through the narrow door frame. A matronly woman with a large plate of towered foods pulls herself back from the doorway. She makes a light-hearted gesture to the small crowd. The children laugh giddily as they huddle together.

    The three floor lodging house has a familiar feeling, even to a stranger like Teven. Breathing in the murky soft scent of frankincense feels like a transcending wave of bittersweet hope. What is he doing here? *A mission? Yes*. His head throbs, as it had since he could remember, which was not long ago at all. He glances up through the large window and to the dimly lit glimmering street. He sees the man in the light robe furiously pedaling and pushing the rusty machine. The machine rocks gently, almost imperceptibly as minute sparks appear and then fade. The man's face turns. Teven can see his gritted teeth and his dark swallowing eyes. *Surely it can't be ...* The others in the lodge do not seem to notice. Teven feels a tight knot in his stomach and tries not to notice himself. He turns around and walks up the creaky stairs. There is an old man sitting next to the upstairs window. He has been tirelessly trying to unlock the window with his feeble fingers. *It must be ready by ten thirty. We are running out of time.* Teven hears another scream in the bedroom behind him. The child has been born, vague cheers suggest. *Ten thirty. No,* the old man says to himself. The old man grasps at Teven's shirt sleeve and pulls him towards the windows. *No, not again, not always like this,* Teven laments but he can't stop himself from turning the key in the window. His pulse quickens as he feels the intensity of the hour. The wind rushes at his face as he pulls the window open. His eyes search hurriedly across the horizon and then knowingly to the street below. To the right, there is the small machine and a woman smiling aimlessly. She is glowing. *What if it's too late?* Teven jumps from the window, willing himself towards the glowing women. He sees the glow dim briefly and then he lands in darkness.

"Machova...!" A soft voice in the distance. Or in the next room. "Machova." The name of the dog. That genial St. Bernard. Teven starts to remember pieces again. He opens his eyes to see the drooping face of Machova. Bringing his fingers to his eye, Teven wipes away the deep sleep of the tunnel. Again, he's gone through, but how many times now? He can only remember fragments. He looks around, finding himself in a quiet room.

"There ye are, Machova," a woman laughs under her breath as she pushes the bedroom door open wider. "Good afternoon, sir." She raises an eyebrow while waiting for his response.

"I'm sorry," Teven says croakily, suppressing a cough with a painful swallow. "I'm a bit confused."

"We found ye last night. Or last morning. Come thinking, it were a whole of last day ye haf been 'ere." Her hand falls over the dog's head and she tousles his white fur with another chuckle. She moves to the doors behind him.

Teven smiles at Machova and sighs, setting off a fit of coughing. "This is a lodgin' house. Expect payment usually, but papa insisted we bring ye in." Teven forces himself to stand, feeling foolish, for remaining in bed for so long, despite his overwhelming sense of tiredness and aching in his head. *Normal for tunnels. Not that I remember any other such travels. Must try to remember something. In time?* "Well, don't jus' stand there, come on through, let's get ye fed." The women motions for Teven to follow her. She steps with requiescence, her pace uninterrupted as Machova pushes past her. The loud trampling of the stairway and the lingering creaking echoes in the adjacent hallway give Teven a sense of nostalgia.

"He mustagun out." *Mitya*, Teven remembers, *the woman's name*. "Likely see t'lady across. Why that'un is stuffier 'an a stuffed teddy bear w'an allergy to wool." At the bottom of the stairs, he immediately grasps towards anything to hold on to. He finds himself a dining chair; Thankfully it stands sturdier than he had imagined it would as he rocks himself through the now increasing waves of nausea. A rectangular screen sits within a large wall of gray bricks. It is alight with actors in bright yellow robes and rudimentary masks.

Mitya continues, "Papa were so sure too. Of ye."

"Yes, I'd be happy to wait for him in your pleasant company. If, that is, it would be no trouble for you." Teven smiles casually while attempting to bring his hand up to clutch the tightness in his chest as subtly as possible.

The first floor of the lodge appears bright and new. The walls seem to sparkle a pale glow in the dim evening light. A soft humming from the window outside draws Teven's attention to the blue blur in the distance. The angle in which he sits at the table allows him to see to the end of the small street. People are gathering there, tall men in blue robes. They are singing now. Teven hears the echoes of their slow song, muffled through the cracked windows.

"The light, the light. The future is light."

5
The First City
9/23/2499 5:37PM

Rhode kneels on the chipped cobblestones, her legs visibly bruised and throbbing from her trek. She watches Nal circle next to a small patch of artificial grass. The relief of escaping from the myrlorx is overpowered by misgiving. It is getting dark and this town has no train station of its own. Her papers and scans are in her suitcase back at the train. Rhode rubs her calves discreetly as other figures pass. She has seen many people following the chanting men, reenacting the first ceremony, in what she now realizes is Fhi, the first city. A small antiquated town, this is the origin of the Thrinaic religion. Rhode recalls stories told to her of the first city; The tall towers were built here to represent the vastness of the Sun. At the time, she had imagined great glass buildings which met the clouds midway. Now, she realizes, the few intact houses that remain standing are no higher than three stories tall.

"First time in t'first?" A man asks as he slows to a stop beside her. Nal jumps onto Rhode's lap and tenses her tiny muscles. "Here for t'ceremony are you?"

"No," Rhode hesitates. Her family had traveled extensively and Rhode is unsure if this had ever been a destination. The man reaches to pet Nal and then jumps back. Ignoring the man's obvious confusion, Rhode briefly explains the incident on the train. Although somewhat taken aback, the man remains oddly calm. Rhode realizes that she hasn't seen any of the other passengers of the train since leaving the woods.

"I'm certain t' s'chána keepers are already at t'train. Ye needn't 'ave left like that. It's not t'way it used to be 'ere."

"I don't think you understand," Rhode tries to start again. "They were coming in from everywhere."

"Yes, it must've ben quite fright'nin' for ye." The man smiles patronizingly. He removes his scroll and skims through multiple news clips. "No nothing is going on in the crescent forest, I'm sure it weren't as bad as all that." His hand jumps up and down over the scroll. Rhode sees the rapidly changing colors reflecting on the man's face. He pauses and a voice comes booming out from the scroll. The voice references myrlorx generally, claiming to have seen a human-like face under their mask. The man scoffs, "Can ye believe that? Hope yer not like tha' up 'n Cymt." He points at her brown dress. "Nonsense," he continues. "I know what they look like. They're different alright." He turns around and continues walking towards the dimming fire, his shoes clodding audibly over the cobblestones. Rhode looks down to her own blackened footprints of her bare feet. "Try t'lodgin' house if ye need a manor for t'night." The man quickens his pace and soon blends into the small crowd. Rhode looks down at her thin brown dress, embarrassed to be so close to the ceremony without formal attire. She reminds herself in vain that her new life is separate from this.

 Rhode stands on her shaking legs, with Nal's long horn gently touching her chin. Turning away from the crowd and their repetitive chanting, she sees the silver and magenta tower in the distance. In the evening light, the colors are subdued. The lights of each window give the entire building a gentle yellow glow. It had seemed nearer on the train. *It must be a few towns over,* she considers. The flickering street light above her goes out and Rhode sees the murky purple in the darkened sky. The street lights are noticeably far apart and the main light of the little town is coming from the ceremony itself. The crowd seems to have stopped, some five hundred yards away. Rhode thinks of what she remembers of such ceremonies. Each town has its own celebration on this day, with fire and drums. It had always seemed large and glorious, regardless of what town in which she had lived. The town elders would read from the Book and, on very special years, children would be allocated to new parents. There were rumors of other things too in the first city.

 Rhode finds herself walking towards the ceremony, her footsteps light over the uneven surface. She pauses at the sight of a child's ball, which appears distinctly unblemished.

She remembers seeing children kicking balls back and forth when she was a child, though this one seems hardly used. She gently touches it with her toe.

"It's much worse 'ere than it used to be." Rhode sees a young woman standing in a doorway of a three story house. Upon hearing the loud voice, Rhode hadn't anticipated the woman's small frame, which is nearly hidden by her oversized pink dress. The woman points to the ball next to Rhode's foot. "Used t'be we'd play for hours when I wa'wee. Not now."

"Sorry?"

"No kids an'more."

"Oh. Maybe this ceremony," Rhode offers politely.

"That'sa'laugh," the woman juts out all at once. "Tha' don' put 'em here anymore." The woman shakes her head. A large dog pokes his head out from behind the woman and looks at Nal. "Ev'n the ligh' cereemony is cheapen'd."

Rhode can see the flames up the road starting to spread as more and more torches are being lit and passed around. She looks back to the woman who is shaking her head in the direction of the ceremony. The dog has disappeared back into the house. Rhode attempts to describe the incident on the train. She pauses as she considers the possibilities of it all. Perhaps others from the train had exited the woods nearer the opposite side of town.

"You came o' t'train? That's 't'awful line there. Always breakin' down and then t'ones left all come 'ere. Good business for papa though." The woman pointed to a sign above the door. Qriau Inn.

6
Ghli
9/23/2499 5:55PM

"He's gone." Kidra stands in front of the empty closet, having swung the door open herself. She couldn't get out of the formal tour of the house. Throughout the long tedious circuit of every inch of the rudimentary new build, Kidra had been running through the possible outcomes to Ghli's discovery in her mind. Luckily, Dant had created a distraction when this room was on display. Having returned from a celebratory drink downstairs, toasting the house, she had thought that she could get Ghli out of here *somehow*. Dant was to make an excuse and then find them.

"What do you mean he's gone?" Ash asks, bemused. Kidra hides her surprise at Ash's sudden presence. "First Dant comes back down insisting I look in the closet... Have you two been snooping around the house? Wasn't the tour enough?"

Kidra frowns. "Dant. What is it that he said?" She turns to look past Ash, only to see the empty hallway. She had expected Dant to come back up by now. She pushes her tightly permed hair away from her face and tries to focus her thoughts.

"Just what I said. What *are* you doing?" Ash tilts her head to her side.

"Nothing. I thought it was Dant coming up the stairs. Inside joke, honey," Kidra replies with the pretense of arrogance. She tries to brush off any suspicion Ash may have, closing the closet with forced aloofness. "I'm so sorry we can't stay. We ... we have to get ready for the ceremony."

"Yes. Dant explained already. He's already on the way." Ash speaks softly as she nods. "I can't wait to see what you two wear tonight. It was a shame last year when you lost your seats to the Je Ahs."

Kidra beams her white teeth at Ash, too focused on Ghli to respond. She needs to find him soon. After rushed goodbyes to other guests, maintaining the charade of seeing them soon enough, she makes her way home. The sharp metal on her ankle has been so placed that her walk is unnatural. She does not dare to quicken her pace, lest be noticed by the widening eyes of passersby. The walks across the busy streets are too often ladened with fawning onlookers.

The majority of Hant's buildings are new, shining things jutting up to the sky at varying angles. Only at particular times of the day will the buildings achieve that beautiful appearance, in which they all are reaching towards the striped Sun. In those moments, when Kidra catches such glimpses, she feels pleasure in her status, in her life in Hant. Despite this, the thought occurs when looking at Hant's few old buildings, makeshift houses, and warehouses, with gold coloured paint filling in the many cracks and holes, that a simple life in them would suit her in some alternative, blithe sort of life. She passes a few of these old wrecks. They are still standing strong, as if they never learned how weak they are.

The reverberations of the Time of the Sun are still felt greatly in this world. She almost feels the dizzying rotation, the whirl around the Sun; The intense heat of the Sun, so large, it could swallow up the earth a million times over. When will it swallow her up too? It is difficult for Kidra to imagine a time when humanity was at the brink of harnessing the full power of the mighty Sun. Despite history being covered with hopeful tales of a promising future, the truth is widely known among the elite of Great Sular. The main continents that became Great Sular and Cymt, along with the central islands, were the only ones to remain after humanity's aborted efforts. The evidence of humanity's failure can be seen to this very day in the blinking espial of the Sun.

But Ghli means more than all of that.

Kidra arrives at the entrance of the striped tower. Standing twenty five floors, it has been the Pi Tels home since their marriage began. Conflict had arisen with the decision to live in the larger city of Hant rather than the first city. There had been a brief period of time when there was talk of restoring that small town to its former glory. The mounting incidents in Crestfall put an end to that. Kidra had been aware of the hushed dialogue between the elders.

She knew her and Dant's best course of action was to remain in Hant. Dant did not put up a fight in any case.

Making her way into the brightly lit central elevator, she feels her body start to shrink. She allows herself to collapse against the handrail behind her and tears begin welling up. *Just find Ghli*. Everything else can wait. She reaches forward to press the button for her floor but stops. She pulls her hand back quickly; Across the panel are dark red smudges. The elevator doors have closed and she feels herself being lifted upwards through the floors. She lets her eyes linger on the small black camera in the upper right corner, the red light inside it blinking slowly. The elevator slows to a halt with a sway and the doors open with a rough clamor. She hears his breathing before she can make out his face.

7
The Inn
9/23/2499 6:17PM

"I didna' even see tha' crittah." Rhode watches from the front table of the living room as Mitya sets up an elaborate feeding device from a refrigerated box with a weighted bottom. The large dog sniffs curiously around Nal's horn. As Nal steps on top of the device, a small section of food is released from the top. This, Mitya had explained, was to avoid irritating her whiskers, although solceros' had none.

This device had been made by Mr. Ish Tin. "Papa's always makin' machineree," Mitya had explained.

Sitting at the circular table, Rhode looks up at this vibrant young woman. Round. The room, too, is oval in shape. It is magnificent in size, though furniture and cheap ornaments are scattered about in no obvious order. Multiple leafs of paper have been dispersed about the table in front of her, haphazardly underneath a dust ridden gas lamp. She feels herself growing frustrated. With no word from the authorities on the train invasion, she is without a clear course of action or means to get to Hant. According to Mitya, there won't be even an acknowledgement of the incident until after the ceremony, if one is to be expected at all. Rhode has no papers to use to travel home and will have to remain locally. This concerns Rhode greatly because Nal will be growing by the day and soon would not be able to be accommodated on a ship. A delay could mean parting ways.

"Ye'll miz t'ceremonee completely if ye don't go now," Mitya says casually. Rhode nods, having already explained that she has no interest in this.

"The Pi Tels will be sure ta be there." Mitya winks, "If ye 're interested in meetin' the big cheeses 'round 're now." Rhode forces a smile and shakes her head. A creak on the stairway causes her to turn her head. Two men are walking down the stairs. The first is an older man with a long white beard and a frail bearing. The second man raises his lowered gaze to smile at Rhode. Both wear matching cloth robes which seem to highlight their dark features.

"Papa! We've anothe' whut caney pay." Mitya nods to Rhode, who shrinks into her chair. The dog has rushed to follow to the older man.

"Yes, I thought as much," the older man chuckles, the broad lines which paint his hollow checks deepening. He looks at Rhode. A fleeting look of revulsion sweeps across his face, which is replaced with the same warm smile as before. After a pause, he faces Mitya again. "We are likely to get the crowd for the midnight meal."

"I'll get ta t'kitzen soon, papa," Mitya says, somewhat blasé. After a look from the older man, Mitya sighs and walks across the room to the kitchen door. The man follows her inside. Mitya's voice can be heard describing Rhode's experience on the train that led her here. Rhode tries in vain to push the thought of the myrlorx out of her mind; Those quivering masks with big bright eyes had been hideously juxtaposed against the uncanny jutting of their jaws and long feeling fingers. The old stories of myrlorx suggest that they had evolved closely from relatives of the orca whales, with their natures being inclined to live within the darkness and silence of the deep sea.

The younger man has positioned himself on a chair across from Rhode and is fastening his gaze to the front window. He points to the large dark shadow across the front window. "I think that's what he was telling me about."

Rhode can hardly believe she hadn't noticed it earlier. She stands to get a better look, her knee nearly giving way from fatigue. Through the window, she sees a large machine with a central padded seat and two long handles. Gears of all sizes protrude from all sides. "What is it?"

"I still don't quite know right now. I've seen this kind of thing before, I know that much." He explains that he had arrived last night and has struggled with his memory due to his strenuous journey here. "My memory is coming back in bits and pieces. Mr. Ish Tin has been quite helpful. That is, I know he's trying. But it's nothing to what you've been through, I'm sure. Quite harrowing."

Rhode ponders over Teven's voice. She had noticed that Mr. Ish Tin, too, spoke without a distinct regional accent that the smaller towns of the land are famous for.

"You'll see it in action now, kid. This is an important night." The old man, Mr. Ish Tin, walks back into the dining room, holding a large glass bottle and several glasses.

"Are you going to set it up?" Teven asks politely.

"I'm sorry," Rhode forces herself to interrupt. She kneels to the floor and picks up a sleeping Nal. "Ms. Mitya said that I could rent a room on credit. Shall I retire there for the night and leave you to it?"

"Oh, I'm afraid we can't go without you." The old man chuckles gently. Looking at Teven now, he says "Oh yes, boy. You *must* understand your place in this. Has your motion sickness settled yet?"

"Yes," Teven states apprehensively.

"Then come on, boy, we'll see the machine up close." Mr. Ish Tin leaves the bottle and glasses on the table and smiles at Rhode. "You too then. Mitya hasn't made your bed yet."

Rhode feels obliged to follow although she is ambivalent towards his fervor. Rhode notices the front door has a keyhole; The uncommon locking system has virtually been replaced by automated biometric doors. They walk to the front of the house and stand before the machine. It seems even larger than it did from inside. Still carrying Nal, Rhode watches the man instruct Teven on how to operate the machine. The gears start turning and sparks fly off in all directions. Rhode takes a step back. Mr. Ish Tin urges Teven to quicken his pedaling while he fastens a new electrical cord to the machine.

"What is this?" Rhode asks.

"Time," Mr. Ish Tin replies.

8
Bound
9/23/2499 6:51PM

Kidra opens her eyes, wincing at the pain behind them. The memories of what had happened come rushing back to her. Dant had grabbed her, pulled her from the elevator. He was covered in warm, wet blood. He hadn't said a word. When she tried to push him away he held her tighter and shoved a wet cloth into her mouth. Before she could remove it, her consciousness started to drift away. He had taken her, carried her, down the stairway of the tall building. For many floors, her consciousness drifted before finally disappearing completely. Now on her side, her arms and legs bound. She hears voices from far away, very far. Thoughts float around her brain of what he may have done. Dant.

    Her thoughts drift back to their first year of marriage. It had been difficult for her to tolerate being so near to him so often. She inferred that this feeling was to be expected in the context of arranged marriages. When her former classmate had invited Kidra to her wedding on the most eastern of the Njuyut Islands, just off the coast of Cymt, Kidra had been more than eager to attend, and assuredly alone. While the elders had decided soon after she had left that she must return, she did not receive this letter for some days. Once she had, she was sure to make her way leisurely towards the boat. There had been an unusual amount of Sun on the island. On her way, she saw a young man. They shared a laugh and soon found themselves walking in the same direction. She had sensed pure admiration in him. Kidra had missed this sort of attention dearly. They neared the beach on which her friend was due to be married the following day. Somehow this turned into more laughter and their arms touched. She felt reckless, allowing herself to be so close when she knew she lacked the antibodies necessary to be so imprudent on this island. A moment of silence and Kidra felt herself being pulled gently towards the man. He pushed his limp lips on hers and she felt mildly nauseated. Forcing herself away, she found herself walking onwards, to find her way to the boat, wishing she had stayed. She had thought about becoming pregnant by the man and what a world like that would be. The elders would have to hide this pregnancy and pretend to offer the child to her in a ceremony. After all, it would certainly be an unnatural occurrence after all these years for someone to bear a child. At the time, Kidra had been unsure if they would ever receive a child even with their current standing. Even then, the child allocation rates had been declining.

 She walked across the sand and saw a small cat, perhaps a kitten, running across the water's edge. She had tensed as it ran into a crashing wave. Another larger cat was quick to follow. Both ran towards the long grass, out of Kidra's eyesite. The shouts of a woman had caused her to turn. The woman running towards her was middle aged and wore a headscarf tying her graying hair back behind her head. Kidra had tried to ascertain if the cats were hers but the woman's accent was quite strong; She spoke only in broken Sularian. The woman was quick to compliment Kidra and had asked her to help her bring the cats home. Kidra had already been inclined to delay her boat trip so she agreed. The woman said that she did not live far away, so Kidra followed her to her. The long path to the hut was winding. The overgrown weeds sticking out from all angles made the house all the more confining. The woman showed Kidra the other cats she had at her home and stressed how much she missed those two that ran off. Kidra had felt a rush of pride at the woman's attention which quickly turned into deep unease when the woman started asking her to touch her belongings. When Kidra refused, the woman's face became dark and sinister. The woman began shouting terrible things at Kidra. Kidra backed away and said in Njuyuti "I wish you luck," which was what she had always been taught to say to the meager. The woman shouted, angrier, and Kidra hurried away. She rushed forward, maneuvering herself out from the maze of long grass. When she was finally free, she walked promptly towards the large mass of the ship in the distance. She felt the need to look over her shoulder for the rest of the trip. The waving voyage home across the ocean was long and she had many nights on the thin bed within the little private cabin to indulge in her fears.

She lies alone again, the voices around her seeming hollow and far away. She winces at the thought of Ghli. Dant's blood soaked hands surely meant one thing. Trying to clear her croaky throat, she struggles with the heavy soreness in her throat. Her hands, she realizes, are bound loosely and she tries to free herself. The rope had been tied in an unsophisticated manner and she is able to push one finger back painfully to loosen it sufficiently; One hand slips out and then the other. Pulling her feet towards her she begins winding the more arduous knot. Unable to meet the same success, she finds the knife kept in her ankle holster and cuts through it.

A door in the room reveals itself with a slit of light. The sound of whispering voices seep through the walls. The room itself seems unfamiliar. Kidra stumbles lightly as she stands up, her gown, amassed with dried blood, stiff against her skin. The voices have quietened completely now and there is a thick tension in the air. There is a creak and Kidra's heart jumps. As she tenses her body, she realizes the sound was from the floorboards beneath her. An anger builds up inside and she resolves to move forward, unafraid. She reaches out to the door and thrusts it open. A gasp escapes her mouth as her eyes fix on the fire.

9
The Cave
9/23/2499 6:59PM

There is only darkness in front of Teven. He is lying flat on his stomach with his arms to his sides. He tries to move his arms but finds strong resistance. Twisting his hands around, he can feel sharp cold rocks at his fingertips. He breathes in deeply and feels a sharp pain on his ribs. After a moment of sheer panic, he resolves to breathe in slow and shallow breaths. The pain in his ribs lessens but does not disappear. He moves his feet and attempts to push himself forward against the slippery surface. Inch by inch, he hopes to find a widening in the enclosed space. Teven is unsure if his eyes are starting to adjust to the pitch black or if his mind is playing tricks on him. He thinks he can see a rocky wall in front of him and a hint of a grin embedded in it. The dripping water along the walls seems to shine with a delicate green.

The last thing he remembers is pedaling the stationary machine. He hadn't been able to stop himself. His thoughts flashback to the old man and the familiar feeling he had at their first meeting. The man's long gray beard highlighted his grand smile as he entered the inn. His chuckle had stopped abruptly when his eyes met Teven's. That somber stare was soon replaced with another welcoming smile.

"Mitya, you managed to wake him up then?' Mr. Ish Tin had put his right hand forward to Teven, which Teven tentatively obliged with a shake. "Those time tunnels leave a keen headache behind, don't they?" After a moment of pleasantries, Mr. Ish Tin asked Teven about his mission. Teven confided that the details remained repressed. The strong sense of familiarity led Teven to believe that the two knew each other well.

"Oh, no, boy. We've not met one another before, per se. But I know how you came to travel here." Mr. Ish Tin had sat down and was pouring himself a drink from a bottle of red liquid, lingering for the final drop to plunge into a series of ripples. "Let me start again for you. From the beginning. Or perhaps I should show you." The old man had said when he saw Teven's confusion.

Suddenly, Teven slips forward on the inclivity of the cave floor. He tries to brace himself, but moving face first, he knows there is little he could do. The pounding in his ears surge as he sees a gleam of light.

10
The Ceremony
9/23/2499 7:02PM

The reflection of the fire luminates over the thick plastic covering. The oracle guides a trolley of wrapped goods towards the center of the chanting ceremony. The four Thrinaic elders in blue robes and lace headdresses lead the chanting. They pass a flaming torch back and forth between them as the crowd watches. One elder pulls back a small curtain to reveal a small child. The crowd gasps. A woman far back in the crowd exclaims "At last!" The child remains still, her eyes wide. Another elder removes the items from the trolley and begins to unwrap the contents. He gloves his hands and attaches a syringe to a large red bag with a thick central tubing. The oracle pulls the child from the waist and inspect her hand before holding her arm out. Her small arm has a large cannula sticking out. The child cries in fear and tries to resist. The remaining elders move to hold her still while the tubing is secured. The crowd cheers softly.

Rhode watches from the back of the large crowd, staring upwards at the immense projection of the ceremony just above the elders. Rhode had picked up a turquoise cloak from the ground near the ceremony and now holds it tightly against her body so as to not attract attention as an outsider; Although the night brings cold air, the heat of the fiery ceremonies often leaves the onlookers sweltering. Having left the inn with Nal, fearing the old man's manic talk of the machine, she had sought solace in the nameless mass of people cumulated around the event.

"Once enough electricity is generated," Mr. Ish Tin had explained, "And the time is upon us, all the tunnels of time will be there and ready for the taking." Rhode had felt her body tense and she stepped further back from the machine.

"First you must reenact the first travel of 15 years ago, you must put yourself in that state and Teven in his, so you must act accordingly in order to split the channels of time."

It is all too much for Rhode, "No, wait, you're talking of time motion." Then it clicks for her. Time motion is a new phenomenon of recent years. Although deemed by some to be an achievement, it has failed to garner the attention or respect of the elders in Great Sular or Cymt.

"Of course."

Teven had continued pedaling, almost in a trance. A small yellow glow appeared amongst the erratic sparks. "You see, the portal is beginning to form. Only tonight, you see, and only if we move quickly. One hundred and twenty miles per hour, at least. But we can travel for days then. I remember it so well." Mr. Ish Tin had stared at Rhode, wide eyed. The intensity was frightening. Rhode had run away then. She soon found herself comforted as she grew closer to the large crowd. She had slipped into it with ease, remembering the sensations of her childhood; The familiar smells of burnt wood and the sounds of familiar songs and words of refreshing comradery are just the same.

The elder to the right of the circle thrusts the torch into the air and exclaims, "Iltt!" The crowd buzzes in collective revulsion. He stands on top of a wooden box, the conflagration box, which he would soon add to the fire. "The first Thrinaic, Trem, came upon a beautiful woman." The elder's voice trembles with command. Rhode knows this story well. "He was sitting under a tree, the last of the trees to be cut to create the first city, when he felt a small branch fall onto his shoulder. He looked and saw her. She had flowing yellow hair and beautiful white lips. She slipped down from the tree and ran from him. Weary from axing the land's trees, he did not follow her. Instead, he left the tree standing and returned the next day. On close inspection of the tree, he saw her to be hiding on the highest branch, burying herself beneath the autumn leaves. He shook the bottom branch and the rest of the tree waved. Leaves and branches started to fall and soon the woman made her way down the tree. Again she ran, but Trem was strong and he chased her capably. She ran to a cave and disappeared into a small hole. Trem cursed the woman for fleeing from him. But again he left the tree, in the hopes of finding her there the next day. Trem was correct. Again, he saw her back in the tree, but this time he assembled a circle of fire around the tree so the woman could not escape. He shook the tree again and he saw her move down the tree. When she saw she was indeed trapped, her eyes became large and sad. She posed as a gift from God. Trem made her his bride and he built the first city with her. But in time he saw the evil in her." The elder moves with his torch towards the child. "After he learned of The Devil's Blood, he cut her to pieces and let her blood drain into a large bowl. He set fire to the tree and dug a hole for the remains of her body. *Then*, he let her blood drip onto the fire, cleansing her spirit itself.

"Let us not forget Iltt, the insidious one! The first myrlorx!" The crowd roars together and Rhode feels a shout escape her throat. The elder steps down from the box, removes the empty bags from the transfusion, and alights it with his flame. The child is crying and collapses to the ground. Rhode sees another man step forward from the crowd. He has dark thinning hair and a pale complexion. The man, with the elders around him, holds the girl still. The oracle takes out the siyalline suit and begins the application of the new skin. Rhode touches her arm, feeling the smooth siyalline of her own. The pain it inflicts as the pin prick gripping spikes pierce through one's natural skin is fleeting but intense. Over a period of weeks it stretches over and molds perfectly to the body while the spikes loosen and break apart in the bloodstream. The crowd is silent. The oracle then takes out an implant gun and presses it to the back of her head. The girl squirms and lets out a single shriek as the oracle implants the microchip into her spine. In time, the body adapts and the microchip within the spinal cord can enact its effects on the internal organs; Shrinking, the organs become more efficient, less active. The man takes the child back to the crowd which cheers around him again.

There is a collective euphoria within the crowd. Statements of joy, regarding the new child being allotted, are whispered excitedly around Rhode. All of the chanting has stopped and the sounds in the crowd lessen until there is almost silence. The crackling of the fires and hiss of smoke spark a calm in the crowd. Rhode closes her eyes and feels a peace inside of her that she had long forgotten about. She remembers being a child and being lost within a throng such as this. The fear she had experienced in that moment had soon been surmounted by the serenity of worship.

Rhode feels Nal tense herself in her arms. Rhode looks up and sees a disturbance at the edge of the crowd. Someone screams and hands raise. Rhode is jostled back and nearly loses her footing. To Rhode's horror, she sees first one then many myrlorx rushing towards the elders. From afar, she can see how hunched their bodies stood, how vulgar they appeared in their tawny robes. Rhode has never known a myrlorx to venture to a ceremony before. They are known to have a great fear of fire. Other faces in the crowd, too, showed deep dismay. She sees the elders stand tall against the myrlorx, who moved ever closer. Rhode breathes in sharply as she sees an elder snatch a mask from one of the myrlorx face and throw it to the ground. Rhode looked away, afraid to see its distorted features. She hears another scream and a chill runs down her body. The myrlorx began attacking the elders and the crowd, opening their jaws unnaturally wide to hinge their mouths against their victims.

Rhode holds Nal close and turns to run. The crowd around her disperse and torches are dropped haphazardly. Rhode does not look back as she hears more screams, this time from the elders. Suddenly, a myrlorx appears before her. Rhode slows to a halt and loses her balance. Nal falls from her arms and races away back towards the inn. Rhode looks up to see that she is surrounded by myrlorx reaching down towards her. She grabs the end of one's long damp robe and pulls with all her might as she brings her limbs towards herself. The myrlorx falls backwards and Rhode pushes herself up to her feet to continue her escape. Again, she feels the long fingers of the myrlorx on her body and she is pulled back. She breaks her fall with her wrists and feels the warm sensation of blood. The people from the crowd are running in multiple directions and Rhode sees someone make contact with another myrlorx in front of her. In the commotion, she crawls between two robed figures and starts running again. She sees Nal in the distance and quickens her pace. Solceros are known to run one hundred and twenty miles per hour at full speed. Rhode only hopes Nal will slow her pace. She feels relief as Nal turns towards the inn, but as Nal runs towards the glowing light of the machine, she disappears in a flash of green light.

11
The Evasion
9/23/2499 7:29PM

41

Sweat glistens on Dant's forehead as the whirling fire encloses around him. A myrlorx runs towards him, its mouth screaming below its melting mask. The heat of the fire has caused the mask to display an even more macabre form, liquescent. Before he can react, the young child is ripped from his arms. He reaches forward in a rage but the myrlorx and the child recede into the wall of flames. Dant swings around and kicks the conflagration box, which overturns and splits open. He picks up an abandoned veil from the ground, alights it with a wild flame, and lets it fall onto the box as he scrambles away. He feels the scalding licks of the fire against his arms and exhales heavily. The sound of a rotelcopter whirrs above. The s'chána keepers have arrived. *At last*. Dant hadn't anticipated such an attack, though news of lesser offenses have been filtering through to Kidra and him for some time. He feels a firm hand grasp his upper arm and he pulls away.

"Come, Dant," Bal Tel, Dant's father and the third oracle priest of Great Sular, shouts against the screaming blaze. "Let the myrlorx burn this town to the ground!"

Bal leads Dant away from the ruins of the ceremony and the advancing myrlorx and towards a gated house. Stopping, Bal removes a key fob from his blue robe and unlocks the gate. Dant sees a large glowing machine outside the house across from them. Bal enters a small black elliptical vehicle and before Dant can consider the machine any further, he follows suit. The two travel swiftly through the abandoned streets of the town's eastern quarter. Dant turns back to see the diminishing light of the town behind them from the tinted dome windows. The thrust vehicle has already been set to its route but Dant cannot see the destination on the translucent screen around them. He grimaces as he senses where they are going.

"That was nearly as bad as your first allotting," Bal grinned smugly. "I'm sorry. Your *only* allotting."

"This is a disaster."

"It's to be expected, Dant." Bal shakes his head. "You want to be an elder but you can't even deal with something like this."

Dant clenches his teeth and looks out the window at the rapidly passing houses and trees. He had worked hard on the prototype of the bridge. His plan to literally bridge the conflicting nations had impressed the elders and prompted his nomination to be made an elder himself. "A rubbish idea" his father had called it dismissively. Dant knows it to be true.

"People live in that archipelago. You just don't understand the world. But that's you. You don't want to know," Bal scowls at Dant, who remains silent. *You're one to talk,* Dant thinks, mouthing the words to himself. Bal himself has frequently taken full responsibility for the Mass Relegation. Six years ago, the Mass Relegation seemed like the perfect solution to the heavy external debt owed to Cymt. Up until last year, it had been viewed as a favorable decision amongst the Sularians, but ever since the population drought, the news coverage has been less than sympathetic. Unfortunately, the hit to the populations of the smaller towns was unprecedented with more and more incidents of myrlorx being discovered in the pre-ceremony blood tests. "You should have rescued some of that blood. It looked like you had a few litres in that box," Bal adds. Dant doesn't reply. He thinks back to Kidra, her body weak and limp from the blood loss. "We'll need some for a new allotting ceremony for you."

"There won't be more children available for months,' Dant replies haughtily. "Anyway, they won't put me up for another one now."

"That's just what I'm talking about, Dant. See, you're in over your head with this eldership campaign."

The vehicle slows and starts to roll vertically up a tall building. Dant braces his body just too late and falls backwards against the dome window. Bal tuts his tongue and looks away.

The vehicle arrives at last on Dant's large semi circular balcony on the twenty fifth floor of the striped building. They exit the vehicle, which lowers itself back down immediately. Dant presses his finger against the glass window and the sliding doors open. Dant enters quickly and sits down on the long slim L-shaped couch. He sighs as he hears Bal, who has been jolted by the site of the room, shout. Thick patches of blood are pooled around the floor and bloody fingerprints have been smeared across two of the walls. A bloodstained knife sits on the table in front of Dant.

"God, Dant. What happened? What have you done?"

"I had to take care of something." Dant picks up a knife and runs his finger against the blade. "And I did."

"Put that thing down, you idiot."

Dant compliantly places the knife back on the table.

He explains to Bal what had happened at the La Kes', having attended a pre-ceremony party of-sorts. "We brought Ghli."

"Well, that was a mistake," Bal says without missing a beat.

"Yes, I know," Dant mumbles. "Kidra wouldn't leave him. She was afraid of how it would look."

"Typical."

"Well, you see. Ghli had been... well you know what he was like. And at the party... Well, just the worst thing happened." Bal fixes his eyes on Dant. "He had been trying to cover his face, everything made him cough. Then I look at him and ... the redness in his face.. he might as well have been wearing one of those masks. You know." Bal's face drops. "Anyway, I pulled him away before anyone could see and we locked him in an upstairs closet, of all places."

Dant goes on to explain how he and Kidra had struggled with Ghli's indisposition. Dant had insisted Kidra leave the room so he could persuade Ghli to leave by some other means. Kidra was fuming and full of sarcastic remarks to Dant but was desperate enough to agree. Within that time, he had snuck Ghli out of the bedroom window and convinced him to meet him at home. He walked downstairs, excused himself, and then left. He met Ghli in the apartment as planned and that's when he did it.

"Well?" Bal asks.

Dant shrugs.

"So you did what needed to be done?"

Dant nods.

"We need to get on top of this."

"I *am*, father."

Bal shakes his head and heads for the door. Dant glances at the knife again and then quickly looks away.

"I'll speak to you after I sort this out, Dant." Bal exits through the main door.

Dant stands and looks out the large windows at the dark night before him. He wonders if Ghli has managed to escape to the Crescent Forest.

12

The Travel
9/23/2499 7:50PM

Rhode, having returned to the inn, is staring through the window at the light of the machine, now an impossibly bright flash of green. The chaos of the ceremony seems far away, despite the fire from the central crowd continuing to spread towards the inn in crackling embers.

"We need you now. You must save Teven. Like your little solceros, he is bounding through time. Or he should be. I fear he has become trapped in the tunnel and the repercussions of that could be catastrophic." Mr. Ish Tin's deep set brown eyes are greatly widened and he taps his long fingers against the dining table in a compulsive manner.

"What? Where is Nal?"

"You must enter the portal to find her." Mr. Ish Tin pours two glasses of a lohqra liquid and pushes one towards Rhode.

"Why me?"

"I've seen you--" Mr. Ish Tin stops suddenly. "I can't explain how I know. But time is of the essence."

Rhode crosses her arms and looks down at the nutrient drink.

"*Please*," Mr. Ish Tin pressed. "It must be you and it must be now."

Rhode looks at the machine again. The pulsating light of the approaching flames are reflected in the dirty window. She thinks of Nal and her heart aches. She takes a sip of the liquid and nods slowly. Mr. Ish Tin turns hurriedly to the staircase. Rhode follows him to the top landing and Mr. Ish Tin fiddles with an old fashioned lock and key at the bottom of the window.

"There." He says, unable to control the timber of his voice. "This is high enough to reach sufficient speed. Just make sure you land within the glow. Not that you'd likely die should you miss," he adds grimacing. An intense whooshing sound becomes audible as he shoves the window open. Rhode's eyes are drawn to a moving spot light following a running myrlorx. A gunshot is heard and the myrlorx collapses. Rhode looks down at the pulsating light of the machine and grips the window frame. *This is mad!* "Now," Mr. Ish Tin urges, smiling. "Before you change your mind." And with that he pushes her head through the window and shoves her lower half forward in a flip. Rhode falls towards the machine and before she realizes what has happened as the glow of the machine intensifies. The light fades in a smog and Rhode finds herself standing upright within a crevice of a large stone wall. The only light coming in is from a small crack above her. In a moment of claustrophobia, she screams. The sound ricochets against the walls and pierce into her ear drums. She flinches.

"Is that you?" A soft voice from above calls out. *Is that Teven?*

"Teven?" Rhode's voice trembles.

"Yeah, it's me. I'm... I'm trapped over here."

"What happened? Where am I?"

"It is Rhode, isn't it?"

"Rhode, yes."

"Rhode, can you hear from my voice where I am?"

Rhode looks up. Her hands search against the wet stone in front of her for a groove that she can use to climb upwards towards Teven's voice. As soon as she feels her fingers grip around a groove, she feels it slip away. Frustrated, she shouts, "I'm trapped down here. I..." She feels a placid breeze on her right arm. Although the darkness to her right triggers some trepidation, Rhode squeezes her body through the large opening. The breeze grows into a wind and she feels the erosion of the stones around her. The stone on either side of her body gives and she finds herself freed. Her eyes adjust to the large pit room and they focus on the delicate stalactites overheard that seem to sparkle with their own brilliant light.

"Are you near?" She hears Teven ask. An echo bounces from above and she sees his shoulder wedged above a large rock. She climbs over the stone and manages to get a firm grip on his shoulder.

"Can you pull me out from here?"

"Yes, I think so."

"Well, get to it. Before you change your mind."

Luckily, the stone surrounding Teven is covered in a slippery mud that allows Rhode to pull him forward and free his left arm. With that, Teven repositions himself and is able to pull himself out fully into the room. He breathes in and, in a contiguous movement, allows his chest to expand to its full width. Rhode does the same, realizing the tight feeling on her chest is from the pressure of the stone.

"What is this place?" Rhode asks as she looks again at the magnificent room. "Is this really time?"

"Yes. I remember it well again, thankfully." Teven smiles. "Just in time, too."

"I need to find Nal, now."

"The solceros. Of course, it won't be difficult to find her here. Not as she gets bigger."

Bigger? How long will we be trapped here for? Rhode tenses and tries to push the image of wandering in time for years on end from her mind. The tightness she felt earlier was bad enough. "How will we get out of here?" Rhode asks. "Can Mr. Ish Tin control the machine?"

"I'll get back alright. I remember now."

Rhode walks slowly towards the main wall of the room. She sees that there are multiple tunnels and crevices leading off from the large room. "What did he tell you? What is his goal?"

"It's a long story." Teven laughs gently and walks confidently across the room towards her.

Suddenly, Teven's face changes. Teven tries to hit Rhode with a stone within the small cavern. Rhode ducks and falls to the ground. Teven advances, his large feet heavy against the ground beneath them. Bewildered, Rhode crawls away, grasping at the ground in front of her, urging it to pull her away. She sees a narrow gap to her left and she pushes her body inside. She has to exhale air from her lungs to fit, but she manages to squeeze herself through. She hears Teven's hands reaching behind her, but soon the echoes of his grunts cease.

"Time comes full circle, Rhode," he shouts through the gap. "I'll get to you through another tunnel. It's just a matter of time."

Rhode pushes forward, struggling to control her quickened breathing.

"He told me to bring back your lifeless body. I'll have that to look forward to."

13
The Woods
9/23/2499 9:43PM

Kidra weakly stumbles through the woods. Her breathing is heavy and her body feels like it is still burning. Her hands are completely deformed from the fire. Dant had been waiting outside the little room with two elders. She had tried to fight back but was impossibly weak. The twinge in her arm made her understand why. While she had been unconscious, Dant had taken her blood to use for an allotting ceremony. To her horror, she was then forced into the conflagration box, in order to be burned at the ceremony's end. As the ceremony began, she had banged against the interior of the box until she lost consciousness. She awoke to the heat of the fire, realizing the box had been knocked on its side and damaged. She pushed through the crack in the box and ran. She had tried to get as far away as possible from the elders, as Dant has surely turned them against her. She went into the Crescent woods without hesitation, fearing instant death should she remain in the turbulent chaos of Fhi.

The woods have been louder than she thought they would be. Sounds of hooting birds and shifting leaves distract her from her thoughts. The full moon above her gives off only a shallow light and aids the shadows that seem to creep towards her. The warmth of the day replaced by biting cold, she hugs her bare arms around herself. In the distance, she sees a train. She pauses, remembering the multiple incidents that have been occuring along the train line of these woods. Recurrent attacks by the myrlorx have been reported regularly by the s'chána keepers and it has taken a great deal of effort from the elders to keep it from the news cycles. She moves to the side and rests her body against a large tree. She feels the creep of a small insect against her arm and fights the urge to shake it off. She looks back to the train, still and dark. She momentarily considers sleeping in the empty train overnight but quickly realizes that the s'chána keepers could arrive for an inspection at any moment. Resolving to find sufficient cover in the forest behind her, she turns again, and is this time face to face with a myrlorx. She remains still, though fearful thoughts creep into her mind. She knows they have ample reason to seek revenge. She subtly feels with one hand and finds herself holding a thick branch. The mild bumps of the uneven surface of the branch feels like sharp thorns against what remains of her injured hand. As she raises it between herself and the myrlorx, she looks at the mask which covers its face. The large almost sweet eyes startle her and she pauses. The myrlorx reaches towards her. As she tightens her grip on the branch, she feels an acute spasm in her hand and the branch falls. The leaves above her rustle and birds flap away from the tree. Just as she positions herself to flee, it peels back its mask. Its bare face is hauntingly human-like, but for its pale scarred skin that marks the rejection of the chemical resurfacing. Its swollen eyes are dark and familiar. *Ghli.* Nigh with abandon, she hugs him, clutching his dark cloak with her bloodied hands.

"M… mother," Ghli says in a gravelly whisper. Kidra looks down; His skin has become even more rigid and bright. The inflamed and peeling nature of his skin has only worsened since he was first presented to Kidra and Dant at the allotting ceremony sixteen years ago. The beginnings of the transplant rejection process hadn't bothered her in his youth; She hadn't anticipated the gradual paranoia that was being brushed across Great Sular. The myrlorx creatures, or at least their bodies' antigens, somehow responded to the siyalline skin aggressively. Lore told of their new skin being taken from them by the devil. That Ghli's skin was now scarred and bare marks him acutely as a myrlorx.

"Ghli," Kidra holds in tears as she lowers her arms to her sides. "I was sure your father… I didn't want to think about it."

Ghli tenderly holds his mother's injured hands and shakes his head. He points deeper into the woods, past the static train. They walk together, Ghli leading the way, while Kidra's mind rationalizes how the two of them are going to rectify this. After walking for some time, Kidra wobbles and she needs to lean on Ghli to carry on.

Eventually, they arrive at a steep hill. Kidra is unfamiliar with this area, being so far south, although recognises the unkempt wooden gates as typical farmland features. Ghli points to a large square shaped bungalow with a short chimney. Kidra forces herself to follow Ghli up the path towards the house. As they enter the house, the darkness of the room wraps itself around Kidra and she feels herself collapse into Ghli's arms.

When she opens her eyes, she is lying in a bed, over an archaic-looking mattress with thick itchy sheets. Kidra's hands are tightly bandaged. She uses her forearm to feel the hard lump protruding from her left arm. It won't budge. She feels a sudden intense stabbing pain in her lower abdomen and she shuts her eyes tightly. It calms in waves and then disappears completely. As she allows her eyes to open again, they grow more accustomed to the dim light. She sees a cannula attached to her arm, running through a delicate tubing to a dangling bag of red liquid. The door in front of her opens and a woman enters. The woman has wavy hair braided loosely with green ribbon against her head. The woman's slim face and soft features have a calming effect on Kidra.

"Why do you wear myrlorx color? Your new skin is intact." Indeed, despite the poor lighting, the woman's skin shone with a brilliant pink. This is a sharp contrast to the abrogating yellow of her dress.

The woman laughs, "We're all the same here. Honestly, most days around the others I wish I never had a siyalline skin wrapped around me." Kidra shudders at the thought of being bare without her skin and quickly looks down at her hands. Despite the bandaging, Kidra knows that the siyalline had melted off in the fire and her internal musculature is irreparably damaged. Siyalline can withstand a great deal of trauma, usually self repairing in a matter of days, but it has its limitations.

"We've a small portion of lohqra liquid left." The woman sits on the edge of the bed and places her hand next to Kidra's leg. Kidra does not reply, though she hasn't had any nutrient drink for many hours now. She feels herself fold her arms across one another, her hands away from view. "Are you feeling any better? Ghli said you walked here all the way from Fhi. That must have been difficult with that much blood lost." The woman keeps her eyes fixed on Kidra's.

"Where are we?" Kindra asks, though she has a rough idea that they had crossed the threshold of Yandmar forest and are near the South Ghi region.

The woman smiles and reaches over Kidra to the window to her left. The woman pulls back the wool blanket that functions as makeshift curtains and reveals dark evergreens covering a distant hill against the pale blue morning light. Kidra can just make out small white blossoms dispersed amongst the foliage; Magnolia grandiflora are the acclaimed feature of the whole region of the South Ghi. Kidra remembers taking Ghli home after the allotting ceremony.

Dant had been worried about his name due to the close resemblance to Ghi. "I think it's a good thing," Kidra had said to Dant. "It will be an important area in the future. It won't always be an overgrown space of emptiness." Despite the planned projects by the elders, the area remains an expansive wilderness.

"My name is Antrisse. Isse for short." Isse smiles again at Kidra. Kidra feels herself smile back briefly.

"Where is Ghli?"

Isse lowers her gaze. "Ghli needed surgery, too. The skin around his mouth has become too tight. The surgery will help to open his mouth wider to accommodate for the scarred skin. It won't be finished for many hours yet."

Kidra looks away. She had been aware of the makeshift surgeries amongst the myrlorx and knew of the risks. She sees in her mind the grim image of Ghli trying to eat over the last several months. He had tried to hide his agony as she and Dant had tried to ignore it. "Ghli shouldn't be here," she says abruptly.

"He's in more danger with his parents than anyone," Isse says automatically before quickly changing her face to a more sympathetic expression. Kidra remains silent. "I only mean because he is the grandchild of two oracles. They wouldn't allow the publicity of it." Kidra holds her gaze. She knows it is true. That it was everything she had feared day after day. And now the wheels are in motion.

14
Memories
9/24/2499 6:36AM

Rhode continues to crawl through the tight maze of tunnels blindly. The taunting shouts of Teven had long since stopped. Her thoughts have been filled with worry of becoming trapped in the increasingly narrow space, as Teven himself had. Every so often she has seen glimmers of light through coin sized holes in the tunnel. In each, she saw glimpses of impossible things: She has seen the island people of Njuyut walking out from their great red trees and burnt grass towards the thin floating ice on the water's edge; A large solceros horn being used by the elders to keep the myrlorx at a distance; And a crowd of myrlorx thundering over a metal bridge while Teven stands steadfast in front of them. Whether these images, these moments in time, were of past or future, she doesn't know.

Her right arm slips forward and she loses her balance, falling head first into the thin layer of mud beneath her. She breathes out and takes stock. She considers turning around but the passage proves to be much too cramped. She feels a shiver run through her as she considers her predicament. She has no way of return and her knowledge of time tunnels is thoroughly limited. *Where are you Nal?* In her anguish, she feels erratically against the slippery passage walls. As she brushes away a handful of mud, a thin stream of light reveals another moment in time. She peers through, hoping, contrary to chance, to find answers. She sees a young boy with short thick black hair and small brown eyes. *Teven?* He is using a small tool to fasten a small engine into a wooden train toy. The small train scrapes against the hardwood flooring, due to the weight of the engine, and a flame emerges under the small wheel. The child seems to turn to her and stare directly into her. He opens his mouth and screams. Like most of these moments in time, it is short lived, and the stream of light diminishes into the darkness. Rhode pulls herself away and continues her crawl forward in the black nothing in front of her. Digging into the rough stone, she feels the warm sensation of blood spill from her elbows and lets out a small cry. As she hears the supernormal vibration of the echo bouncing from the cave walls, she realizes what she must do. Nearly stumbling over her words, she shouts out into the blackness. The echo comes back hard. She feels her body become rigid from the pain of the roar rolling against the cave walls, but she remains concentrated. She does this again, shouting louder this time. She crawls forward, leaning to the left, where the greatest echo is coming from, and feels along the wall for a passageway. The wall collapses, allowing her to slowly push and pull her body into the empty space. Crawling forward into the passage, she sees a hint of a light far in the distance. She struggles to continue as the passage becomes more and more narrow. Determined to move forward, she tries to control her breathing. Her arms, tightly pressed against the jagged rocks, start to feel numb. Attempting to find the echo again, she tries to shout, but this time can make little more than a whimper.

Eventually she reaches the light and feels the pain of its brightness in her dilated pupils. She eagerly pulls herself from the passage, squinting her eyes in the brilliant room of sparkling flowstone. She takes in a deep breath of the stale air and collapses to the ground. She feels the ground rumbling. *What is happening?* The light becomes unbearable, even with her eyes shut tight. She feels a pulling sensation, bringing her towards the floor, through it. The sound of trubellarps causes Rhode to open her eyes. Before her, a giant orchestra plays on an ornamental terrace, the giant bow of the jialin sweeping across the stage. She turns around to see many soignee persons with delicate glasses of lohqra liquid and jet. She feels herself moving forward, step by step, towards a small pond with a large lotus flower floating at its side.

"Darling!" Rhode squints in the bright Sun to see the approaching figure. A tall woman rushes towards her and puts her hands on Rhode's shoulders. Rhode feels a sharp pain where the woman's hand sits, though this is soon overpowered; Within the pain is the feeling of warmth in the tender embrace. "We can go home soon enough," the woman whispers to her, her hand cupped secretively over one side of her mouth. "Your father has to make a speech for *his* father." Rhode feels an acute stinging to her cheeks, which she realizes, have formed a smile. Another woman approaches and the first stands erect and begins a formal sounding conversation. Rhode's gaze turns down towards the pond where she sees that her reflection is that of a young boy with a single tear sliding down the gentle blush to his cheeks. Suddenly, the image fades and Rhode is pulled backwards, into herself. She finds herself on all fours, staring at the cave floor. Before she can catch her breath, the floor begins to rumble again.

She crawls frantically into the nearest tunnel and to the welcome darkness. The relief fades quickly and she feels a strong compulsion to go back. She comforts herself by glancing back at the room before moving forward. In it, she sees glimpses of another memory. The bright light emerges and fades into the form of an approaching moonlit forest. Appearing nearer and nearer is the body of the myrlorx, nearly hidden underneath an array of white flowers contrasting the crimson blood around his head.

15
Tel Bridge
9/24/2499 8:04AM

Dant stands tall on the blustering entranceway of the bridge. Its skeletal foundation of stainless steel shines crassly in the Sunrise on the eastern coast of Great Sular. Dant had traveled overnight in the rotelcopter with the forth oracle, Dolf Lihe, and the northern elder, Crih Yulah. Pressed together in the doorless pyramid-shaped vehicle, Dant had been eager to reach their destination.

"It should be nearly finished," Oracle Dolf says to Dant. The elder remains silent.

"Yes, it was the natural course of action to accelerate the project." Dant replies. In truth, he is relieved that the incident at the ceremony did not put a halt to the construction. Rather, it spurned the elders to ensure the bridge between Great Sular and Cymt becomes usable as soon as possible.

"We will be able to accommodate intercontinental travel much easier with this," Dolf nods at the bridge, his eyes resting on the snow-covered peaks in the far distance. "This should go a long way towards 'building bridges' with Cymt." He winks at Dant and forces a small laugh.

Dant nods, unconvinced. Despite pitching the project, he knows that the elders of Cymt will be unlikely to accept the idea of long term peace. Once Great Sular's intercounty debt was cleared, following the Mass Relegation, the Cymtian elders' attitude towards Great Sular has steadily worsened in its hostility.

"Come," Dolf whispers nervously to Dant. "We must prepare for the ceremony tonight." It has been decided by the elders counsel that a single mass ceremony would be recorded tonight for live screen viewing, rather than risking any further conflict within district based gatherings.

"Yes, I'm sure it will go to plan," Dant says hesitantly, having to hold his hair in place in the increasing wind.

The elder clears his throat and says "I am more concerned about your... wife."

"A public statement," Dant asserts abruptly.

"A full statement will certainly be required, yes." Elder Crih pauses and looks at the bridge. Construction applicators hover up and down, applying large metal girders with repetitive thuds. "Shall we discuss this further indoors, Dant?"

Dant nods. He follows Crih and Dolf towards a large white tent, which was assembled earlier this morning prior to their arrival. The elders have also organized the build of a large tower which will provide semi-permanent accommodations, but its completion will take another day at least. Dant watches Crih walking hastily towards the tent with his hands behind his back. Dant feels a stab of worry. The northern elder is brother to the late fourth oracle, Daller Pi, Kidra's father and sole parent. He remembers the sound of Kidra's scream when the oracle was shot through the chest three years prior and the years that followed of Kidra's fearful measures against future attacks. *A regrettable time.* He turns his thoughts to tonight's ceremony. "Shall we plan the introduction of my new bride then?" Dant asks as he closes the tent's thin curtain door.

"Bad decision," comes a gruff voice.

Dant tenses. "Father. I didn't realize you were attending the ceremony in person tonight."

"Who says I am?" Bal retorts, sitting back on a commanding wingback chair, arranged in the center of a semicircle of twelve. "But just as I thought, you will be needing some help in planning your speech."

"Father, I'm sure--"

Bal leans back on his chair and removes his scroll. He unwraps it with a certain care that makes Dant grimace.

"There." Bal points to a news report flickering on the scroll.

Dant leans forward to see a still image of Kidra, Ghli, and himself on the screen. Ghli stands somewhat behind Kidra, his face falling into a shadow. The image shrinks and two news anchors stand in the burnt remnants of the first city. Many houses in the background remain standing but appear near to collapse.

"Kidra Pi Tel and son Ghli Pi Tel remain missing. Our thoughts go out to husband and father Dant Pi Tel…" The anchor woman says.

"A missing wife and a suspiciously new bride." Bal shakes his head at Dant and folds his scroll away.

"A presumed dead wife and a grieving husband trying to find joy in his life again." Dant cringes as he says the words. It was only in the early hours of this morning that he had received word of Kidra's survival.

"After one day, how did you manage for so long?" Bal asks under his breath under the glare of the Dolf.

Dant lowers himself to an armchair to the far left of his father. Crih pours a glass of lohqra liquid for each man, insisting on a prayer in consideration to tonight's ceremony.

They drink in silence while the wind beats loudly against the walls of the tent.

Dant thinks back to last night, when he arrived at the apartment to find Ghli. He remembers Ghli bringing his hand to his mouth in a coughing fit and then leaning his hand on the elevator wall. Dant had been shocked at the amount of blood that was on Ghli's hand. His resolve was cemented when they reached the apartment. Although he had had a speech prepared for Ghli, looking into his eyes, Dant was at a loss for words. His eyes fixed themselves on his own reflection in the long glass vase, of the matching set of three, adjacent to the front door. The plastic daffodils inside it seemed to wilt before him. His thoughts had been interrupted by a loud knock at the door. Dant opened the door guardedly. *He must have followed me from the party.* Trigah Ulse, a politician of the small Ves neighborhood had pushed himself inside with spurious charm. Dant had always considered the residents of the port regions in meager social standing and he sneered with antipathy at this display.

"Trigah, I'm afraid now is not a good time for us. Perhaps we can speak after the ceremony," Dant stated with an unnaturally booming delivery.

Trigah looked at Ghli, who shifted awkwardly. "Do not be so ungrateful, Mr. Pi Tel." Trigah contorted his face into a gentle simper. "I am here with a generous offer." Dant felt a panic in his chest. Trigah walked past Dant and stood next to Ghli in the center of the apartment. He stared at Ghli firmly, which prompted Dant to move in front of the door.

"It is quite obvious when one is up close, is it not? Not that you let anyone get too close anymore." Ghli's eyes met Dant's in the silent inference of Trigah's words.

"What do you want?" Dant asked through gritted teeth. Trigah's smile widened and he explained his proposal.

"Let light be us," The elder whispers.

"From those incoming, and not from them," Bal finishes the second day's prayer before Dant has a chance to do so. Dant sighs and crosses one leg over another.

"The ceremony needs to go on. *This* way." Dant explains towards the empty chair across from him.

Bal opens his mouth to speak, but the elder interjects, "The elder counsel have jointly consented to the marriage. Indeed, we need good news for the people."

Bal's eyes focus intently on Dant as Dant's remain fixed on the empty chair. Dant knows what his father is thinking: This sham marriage to a fifteen year old girl is hardly anything to spark the deserved gaiety of the second night of light. Out of the corner of his eye, Dant sees Bal removing the scroll once again from his robe. The voice of the newscaster grows loud as Bal fiddles with the screen.

"The elder counsel have urged the public in their recent statement to remain in their homes. A live coverage of the ceremony will be available to view at six o'clock this evening. We are all certainly hoping for good news tonight in regards to Kidra and Ghli Pi Tel."

Dant pulls his cloak over himself to conceal his hand. In attempting to calm his rapidly beating heart, he had raised his hand to his chest. Voices can be heard from outside the tent, and soon shadows creep across the wall in front of Dant. The tent door opens and a group of four elders and two oracles arrive.

Bal stands from his chair and greets the second oracle. They make the hand gesture of Great Sular oracles and exchange pleasantries. Dant stands and shakes the right hand of each man with the axiomatic respects. The Thrinaic faith started hundreds of years ago. Many of the traditions originate from the previous religions of the area; Thanks and prayer are given to the sky and the Sun. Calmness and separateness are seen as godliness. Safe and clean. The elders and oracles want to keep order in the country. Dant sits back down inelegantly. Two waiters enter with a tray of more lohqra liquid. Dant reaches for a glass and brings it quickly to his lips. The liquid splashes up and a few drops land on the lower portion of Dant's robe. He attempts to wipe it clean but the stain sinks in. As he stares at the small red drops, he is reminded of last night again.

The choice was clear: Find a way to marry Trigah's daughter or Trigah would tell the world Ghli is a myrlorx. "It is something for you to think about." Trigah said as he walked towards the door. "Do not think for too long though, please. My daughter is so looking forward to your answer." Dant glanced to the front door and then to Ghli. He saw more blood drip from Ghli's mouth onto the floor. When Trigah attempted to shift Dant from his path, Dant had grabbed the vase and smashed it against Trigah's head.

Ghli had backed away in fear. Trigah stumbled over the broken glass through to the living room and tried to lean against the wall for support. Dant followed and stabbed Trigah repeatedly with a long shard of glass. Trigah collapsed and writhed about the floor for several minutes until he was still. As Dant stared at the pooling blood on the floor, reaching in thin red lines to meet Ghli's, he realized: *My daughter is so looking forward to your answer.* The daughter must know too. Dant looked at Ghli and urged him to run, to seek refuge in the Crescent Forest. Dant told Ghli to wait in the apartment for ten minutes and then to leave at once. He removed a bottle of solvent from the kitchen cupboard and picked up a small dish cloth. Dant walked out the door and into the communal stairwell. He opened the box to the electrical distribution system. He hesitated before pouring the solvent into the cloth, touching it to the circuit board, and then pulling it back. The lights around him went dark and he had to feel his way back to the elevator. He saw the small flicker of light from the emergency power system in the open elevator door and worriedly approached it. Kidra stood in the elevator, though she did not see him. In a panic, he grabbed her.

Dant is shaken from his thoughts when he sees Bal raise an eyebrow at him. Dant instantly realizes he is sitting on Bal's wingback chair. He stands automatically before rebuking himself for being so subservient.

"Shall we decide on the second night's story?" Asks Dolf.

"I thought it had been decided." An elder queries. "The Betrayal, wasn't it?"

"Ah yes, quite fitting."

16
The Gathering
9/24/2499 5:30PM

The listless remains of the deceased protrude out from under a thick layer of soil. Some of the train passengers are still clinging to their luggage. Kidra hadn't noticed them, scattered ubiquitously, on her journey from the train to the farm house last night. She shudders at the sight. Looking up to the dozen or so myrlorx in front of the old decaying house, she sees many of them picking unripened puurron fruit from the sparse trees. Kidra had awoken from her dreams this morning to find a myrlorx outside the window, rustling, chewing on the puurron fruit of the nearby tree, and staring at her. She has been waiting all day for Ghli's surgery to be complete. With every passing minute, she finds herself anxiously willing herself to interrupt it, stop it, find the location in the house where it is all happening and attack the beastly things.

Her abdomen continues to throb with pain. The grotesque stitching was explained away by Isse to be a necessary surgery from the burns, though Kidra is still horrified at the idea of a myrlorx touching her. The feeling of filth living in close proximity to the myrlorx is bad enough. Already, her skin feels heavy, dirty. She fears asking Isse for so much as a comb, frightened to be given something that would surely belong to a myrlorx. She tries to pat down her wild hair with her scarred wrists once again. They come out of her knotted curls glistening and hot. She thinks back to her tentative meetings with the other residents of this farm; They are temporary nomads, displaced from society and created a makeshift home after obtaining resources from the trains. She tries not to imagine what had transpired to the previous inhabitants of this home.

"There you are." Isse approaches her. "It's important that you stay close." Isse places her hand gently on Kidra's back. Kidra pauses momentarily before pulling herself away. Isse speaks with an accent of someone from Hant. Her air, too, is consistently polished.

"Look, Ghli and I are most grateful, honestly, but we should be leaving at this point."

Isse furrows her brow and then smiles. "You speak for him? I understand." She moves closer to Kidra. "Where will home be for you two now?"

Kidra does not answer. She places her arms under her robe in a small and silent gesture. A myrlorx approaches and Kidra instinctively braces herself. The bright humidity of yesterday has been replaced with a dark foreboding. The ratty gray scarf around the myrlorx' neck nearly blends into the cloudy atmosphere behind them, giving the appearance of their head levitating above. The myrlorx's eyes seem to soften and he raises his face to reveal two gaping holes exposing the teeth within both cheeks. Kidra looks away from the hideous sight and feels a pang of sadness that this is soon to be Ghli's fate. The myrlorx makes several gutterly grunting noises, indistinguishable to Kidra. He motions to Kidra.

"It is an invitation for you to join us for the night gathering prior to our departure." Isse says. When Kidra is silent, Isse explains, "We had planned to leave tonight, for the eastern regions." Kidra pauses again before agreeing to this arrangement. The myrlorx nods and snaps their teeth. Kidra endeavors to remain still, while the myrlorx shuffles away towards the main pathway to the house. "They have precluded their primary means of resources with the raid last night." Isse shakes her head. "My guess is the gathering tonight will provoke a vote to attack the third day of the ceremony."

"How do you understand them?" Kidra asks, her gaze following the myrlorx as his aberrant silhouette dissolves into the darkness.

Isse laughs. "That is a particular one, certainly. Comes from the Darghyong region up north. Quite distinct accents. And of course the tightening of the skin naturally progresses in its own way around the mandible, which no doubt will affect speech." Kidra imagines the sequestered northern regions of Great Sular. With the increasing emergence of myrlorx, it seems they now extend within an immense radius, nearly surrounding the main cities of Great Sular. A short myrlorx with bare feet rushes past Kidra, knocking her slightly off balance. "Shall we go inside to the gathering?"

Kidra finds herself walking towards the front door of the house amongst the rest of the myrlorx. She allows herself another glance at Isse and contemplates what sort of a life she had been trapped within. She wonders how someone born to the myrlorx without developing any affliction would choose to remain an outcast, if that is, indeed, how Isse came to find herself in these circumstances. Inside the house, the group line up to enter the front most room. Kidra's gaze falls to the peeling wallpaper; Once blue and floral, it appears gray with carbon particles of a farmer's blockade. The stench in the room seems to Kidra to be more objectionable than elsewhere in the house.

The myrlorx begin with a summary of yesterday's progress. One myrlorx makes reference to a horn that repels their very skin. This statement is largely ignored by the myrlorx. Isse has to painstakingly translate each comment for Kidra for her to understand and soon Isse resorts to simply summarizing the conversations. The majority of the myrlorx desire war, to combat their unfair treatment. Isse herself appears reluctant, from what Kidra can gather. The myrlorx are seeking to use Kidra's knowledge of the elders and communities of Hant to further their efforts. Kidra is reluctant to speak.

"It seems that paramour of yours has chosen another," Isse says to her.

"What do you mean?" Kidra asks.

"*You,* Kidra, are presumed dead, according to the latest pre-ceremony report by the elders. My guess is that Dant was hesitant to leave himself in a vulnerable position for too long."

"I highly doubt Dant..." Kidra considered this. While it is true that even widowers are discouraged by the elders to remain unmarried, she wouldn't have believed that Dant would ever make such a quick turn around. *Maybe I was cursed by that Njuyuti woman.* Isse makes an excuse for Kidra and the meeting continues. Kidra looks around the room. Two myrlorx stare up at her from seated positions, their arms around one another. Since arriving at the farm house Kidra has noticed that the myrlorx seem to pair up. Marriages in her world are always celebrated and pairing naturally increases the likelihood of being allocated a child. That, in itself, is always said to be altruistic in nature, though approval of the elders is the only real draw. In truth, Kidra did not expect to feel the love for Ghli that she did. Upon hearing a creak over the wooden floor boards by the doorway, she turns to see Ghli enter the group. Her heart becomes alight and then drops when she sees his face. As the gathering concludes, Kidra allows herself to move closer towards Ghli. She reaches for his hands before stopping herself and looks up to his eyes. They are gone.

17
Nal
9/24/2499 6:55PM

The lights crowd her vision such that she seems to be alone with the tall man. Within the silhouette of his profile, she can see just how he has become so recognizable over the past five years. Dant Pi Tel takes her hand and grins towards the invisible audience.

"And thanks to you, my new bride." Dant's gaze remaining forward, he laughs clumsily and allows her hand to fall. To the right of the stage, another man in oracles' robes leads her to another room. She allows herself to slump onto a felt chair with a seashell pattern sewn into the worn blue fabric.

"Just stay here until we call for you," the oracle says nervously. He exits the room, closing the metal door haphazardly and causing it to vibrate.

She stares into the reflection in the shining silver of the door. Her small nose and hollowed cheeks appear the same picture of elegance as they had yesterday. Her eyes however, seem larger, puffier with dilated blood vessels reaching out from themselves.

Rhode emerges from the memory with a gasp. She had thought that she was acclimatizing to the shifting time memories well, but again she is left disbursed. She forces herself to crawl across the small room into another passageway before she becomes caught in another memory. Collapsing into the small nook, she rests her shoulders against the cold moist walls as the stream of light pours from the room behind her.

Rhode closes her eyes and sees Sulsu's wide eyes reflecting back to her once again. When this event occurred, Rhode doesn't know. The subtle nuances that differentiate past, present, and future are lost within the tunnels of time. Sulsu had seemed similar in stature as she had a day ago. Has she been betrothed to Dant Pi Tel even then? She is so young. Rhode feels a panic shoot through her. Clenching her fists, she forces the cascade of memories of Cymt away. She pushes on within the tunnel, forcing herself into an oncoming stream of light, a new memory. With the predictable flash of light, Rhode is engulfed.

The yellowed grass below her blows in the harsh wind. She feels herself rocking gently with the current of air and realizes that she is sitting on a large branch of a puurron tree. The sharp edges of its leaves brush against her face and break up the white sunlight in front of her. A dizziness envelops her as the air begins to settle. She brings her white hands up to her face and feels the cold of her skin. She rests her back against the rough body of the tree.

"Duit, cailin," a voice from below shouts. Rhode has to grasp the tree branch tightly in order to see the origin of the peremptory voice from below. The man below, without lowering his gaze, dismounts from his horse. He speaks again and Rhode surmises that his dialect is that of Old

Sularish. She feels herself reply before she hears the whispered utterance. She lowers one leg and becomes quite faint within herself. She rapidly pulls her leg back up to find delayed relief. The man shouts angrily and his horse snorts loudly at the furor. Rhode feels the tree begin to shake. Her eyes dart to the end of the clusters of thick leaves, one by one falling to exhibit more and more of the naked branch. She loses stability in her grip and slips against the cutting wood. She closes her eyes and waits for the thud of the hard ground to meet her body but there is nothing. Opening her eyes, she sees the dark cave once again. The weakness had felt so real, so paralyzing. Her arms are still shaking as she crawls forward against the rock.

A noise causes Rhode to keep still: A harsh pounding followed by a gentle series of echoes. *Teven?* Rhode closes her eyes to desperately try to feel the source of the sound. *Behind me?* Her shaking intensifies. She frantically pulls herself forward through the rock formation. The tunnel becomes narrower. She can see the end of the tunnel is only a small hole and only darkness appears to await her to the passageway to her left. She continues forward, feeling the sharp rocks break the skin of her arms as her body's involuntary shaking persists. She twists her shoulders so her frame can squeeze through. She pushes through the small hole until her arms are freed. As she squirms the rest of her body through, she feels the bitter cold of a large rock against her cheek. Unable to see, she holds her hands forward and feels the surface of the rock with her fingertips. It surrounds her in all directions. Another thud echoes from behind her. Her breathing deepens and she can feel her ribs pressing against the large rock. She feels her heart pounding in her ears and cannot differentiate this from any further echoes from behind her. In desperation, she reaches upwards and grasps a jutting piece of limestone. She anchors her feet onto the rock and begins to pull herself upwards. As she continues, she thinks she can hear the faint sound of breathing. In the pitch blackness, she doesn't know how far she has climbed. She is aware of sweat accumulating in her hands.

At last, as she reaches to find the rock above her, there is nothing. She lowers her hand and feels a horizontal surface. She pushes down with her bare feet once more and throws herself onto the higher ground. As she allows herself a rest, she hears footsteps in front of her. She trembles again and the footsteps become louder. She feels a warm breath against her cheek and gasps. Her hand moves in front of her to push the intruder away but pauses when she feels the familiar leathery skin. *Nal!* She reaches her arms out and brings Nal towards her, feeling her cold horn against her neck. Nal feels larger than she was, certainly wider than Rhode. *How are we going to get you through these tunnels now?*

In almost a reply, Nal turns around and walks forward, with Rhode holding her horn. They walk forward in the darkness. The ground becomes increasingly uneven but Rhode is relieved that she can walk on two legs again. Soon, the uneven ground becomes one large boulder after another.

Rhode feels Nal jumping with ease from boulder to boulder, but Rhode slips backwards more often than not. In the corner of her eye, she sees a small stream of light. *At last!* Hoping to find her feet, Rhode navigates her way towards the light, despite Nal's seeming attempts to pull her away. The glowing stream seems to be coming from the ground between two boulders. Rhode climbs over each boulder clumsily but eventually reaches the stream of light. She puts both hands on the framing rocks and looks down into the stream. Expecting to see a memory, she looks closer. She can see small particles floating in the stream. Looking up, she sees Nal's face staring at her.

"It's okay, Nal. My eyes just aren't as good as yours," Rhode whispers softly. After attempting unsuccessfully to get her bearings, she resolves to move on. "Ok, Nal. Show me the way again." Nal turns. Rhode pushes herself up against the rock but slips forward. She feels the ground below her crumble. Nal screeches as Rhode slips downwards. Rhode feels herself sliding against small stones, which feel hot in the intense friction. The dark gray in front of her disperses and she finds herself trapped upside down in the ceiling of another large room. She realizes the stream of light is coming from this bright room below. She feels her arms wedged behind her and looks at the hard ground so far below her. She can hear Nal continuing to screech from above. Rhode closes her eyes and frantically tries to think of what to do. When she opens them again, she sees Teven staring up at her from the room below.

18
Leatromach
9/24/2499 11:57PM

Sulsu stares at the bridge in the moonlight. Now nearly finished in its construction, the remaining oil spills into the sea from the floating girders, mixing in chaotic swirls with the increasing drops of rain. Dant comes up beside her, pulling his robe closed tightly against the cold.

"Sulsu, come here. Look away from that, we need to leave." He motions to the spherical thrust vehicle parked in the entrance way of Tel Bridge.

Eventually Sulsu turns and whispers, "I'm coming," in her put-on accent.

She wants to sound like one born and bred in the sophistication of Hant rather than the parasitic port of Ji. "I shouldn't have to tell you again and again." Dant's foot twitches as he speaks. He squirms when he sees her face. She looks at him as if to say, *Why should I listen to you at all? You have no authority over me.* Dant is taken aback. He had continued to hope in the back of his mind that things would be different. That Sulsu would be different, different to Kidra, different to his father. *They're all the same.* He clenches his teeth and begins to grate them against one another until he can feel the vibration in his skull. Sulsu walks past him and into the vehicle without looking back. Dant follows, angrily mouthing his displeasure.

"I have had some thoughts on the ceremony in Cymt." Sulsu says as Dant enters the vehicle. Dant frowns. It has been decided that the third night's ceremony will be conducted in Cymt, should Dant succeed in the dialogues with the Cymt elders. Dant is doing his best to ignore his misgivings about this plan. That the people of Cymt would accept the bridge opening so soon is questionable in and of itself.

"More thoughts?" Dant grumbles.

Sulsu moves her hand to the coordinates on the screen before them. "Where are we going?"

"These things aren't designed to navigate that far. Just set it forward," Dant replies. Sulsu pauses and then pushes her index finger upwards. The vehicle rolls forward and then quickly picks up an accelerating speed. Dant looks away from Sulsu in disgust. "What sort of respectable young girl from Ji would know how to operate a vehicle like this?"

Sulsu throws her head back and laughs heartily. "You wouldn't know, I'm sure."

Dant turns to look at Sulsu. The right side of her face appears in rapid cyclical glows under the blue light of the moon before vanishing anew in the repeating shadows of the bridge's truss.

"I remember your brother, you know." Sulsu says suddenly. Dant feels his entire body tense.

"Everyone remembers Cagh," Dant replies quietly. Sulsu's eyes scan across the bridge to the coarse waves of the ocean below. The walls of water rush upwards against the sides of the bridge and fall again with graceless ease. The rain is coming down harder and the view in front of them is greatly obstructed. After a moment of silence in the vehicle, Dant says, "Ask if you like. Why didn't he stay and have a fuss made of him? Why isn't he going to be the next elder now?"

"Well, on the news he just seemed more ..."

"Yes, I know. Yes, he was. No one made him go. It was his choice." Dant closes his eyes and thinks of their last conversation.

"I need more, Dant. You'll be fine here, but my life is out there." Cagh had smiled his usual smile, full of blithe charisma.

"Have you spoken to Father?" Dant had asked, knowing full well that their fathers opinion meant nothing to Cagh. And that Cagh's meant everything to their father.

"He knows my intentions."

Dant had clasped his hands behind his back and pushed his feet into the ceramic floors. In those weeks leading up to the Mass Relegation, tensions had run high between the oracles and the elders of Great Sular. The elders, against the advice of the oracles, had wanted to restrict tourism to the Njuyut Islands and Cymt until the tensions between Great Sular and Cymt settled. Cagh, who had desperately wanted to travel far and wide, past the Njuyut Islands and past the castle of Cymt, left in a lone boat without the knowledge or approval of the elders.

Dant lets a sigh escape his purses lips. "Yes, I stayed ... and stepped up to the task. It was the honorable thing."

"I would think it would only be honorable if you were any good at it." Dant's hand moves to the stain on his robe, scratching at the dried liquid while he contemplates Sulsu's words.

Suddenly, a large wave crashes against the front of the vehicle, pushing them back and swerving them to a stop. The vehicle wobbles slightly before moving forward again, but this time instead of heading across the bridge, it moves off center towards the bridge's edge.

"Stop this thing!" Dant presses his hands into the screen but it remains clear.

"Where's the emergency button?" Sulsu frantically reaches under the screen to find nothing. The vehicle crashes into a metal railing and Dant and Sulsu are jolted against one another. Dant's vision darkens into black before he passes out.

He wakes with a start to a loud creaking sound. Looking to his right, he sees Sulsu unconscious against the rest stand of the vehicle. In the background, the ocean waves seem closer still. In an instant, he sees where they are: the vehicle is barely balanced on the edge of the bridge. He feels the lowering and raising of the vehicle in a delicate battle between gravity and mass. Dant stiffens his body and reaches for the opening of the door. Slowly, he pushes it upwards, stopping at each movement of the vehicle. A torrent of rain spills into the vehicle and Dant jumps out and onto the cold metal bridge.

He stares back at Sulsu, unconscious in the vehicle, as it tilts up and down with vicious indifference. He resolves to try to remove her from the vehicle. Reaching forward, he unlocks her left shoulder brace. He feels the vehicle tipping greater and he pulls back. The vehicle lowers and then raises again. He sees the build up of water accumulating on the floor of the vehicle. He again reaches towards Sulsu, but cannot reach her right brace. He pulls at her left arm hard.

"What happened?" Sulsu groans.

"You need to get out." Dant struggles to speak; Each breath in the heavy rain continues to fill his mouth with salty water.

"Were you just going to let me fall? Get me outta 'ere!" Before Dant can take any further action, Sulsu removes her remaining shoulder brace and crawls out of the vehicle. She grabs hold of Dant's legs as the vehicle slides down and falls out of sight. Dant loses his balance and falls backwards against the bridge. He hears a crash in the ocean below. Sulsu stands, already soaked in the heavy rainfall. She looks across the bridge towards the mountains of Cymt far off in the distance.

"It will be an hour on foot to get back, but at least two dozen to Cymt." Dant says.

"We can't walk in this rain," Sulsu spits.

"Stay if you want to." Dant walks back towards Great Sular. Sulsu begins to shiver and she rushes to follow. Dant gently smiles to himself.

"They will send someone for us, you know."

"I'm sure you're right." Dant sighs. The metal bridge is pooling with water. Dant can feel the freezing liquid in his shoes, submerging his toes.

"Some wedding night."

Dant looks at Sulsu. A thin cloud has covered the moon and has shaded its reflective light. The darkness over Sulsu's face seems more playful than sinister, but only just. "Yes, I know," Dant replies in a robotic tone.

"I don't know why you're the one behaving so contrary."

"Me? You've been behaving like a spoiled brat."

"I'm sorry." Sulsu stops in her tracks. Dant continues walking for a moment and then turns to face Sulsu. "I am so sorry. It must be so difficult for you. Murdering my father. Rushing to tell me before yesterday's ceremony and then tricking me into marrying you to keep me quiet. Your life must be so challenging."

"Yes, it is. And you've no idea. No idea at all. And you - you're lucky to be here--."

"My father was in line to be an elder too!"

"--with your sarcastic little comments. I'm sure they called you witty in that cesspool you came from!"

Sulsu stops and stares over Dant's shoulder. He hopes he has finally quietened her, but soon he sees a light in his peripheral vision. He turns and sees a large thrust vehicle moving towards them with its central beam pointing forward. He squints to make out Bal standing in its center. Dant mutters a curse under her breath. Sulsu rushes past Dant, giving him a lingering critical look on her way to the vehicle.

"Get in, girl," Bal says as he steps out of the vehicle and walks towards Dant. "I'm not surprised, in all your planning of this bridge, you didn't even take the water into account. Precipitation can't just be an afterthought, Dant."

"Were you sitting there just waiting for the alarm from the vehicle?" Dant asks bitterly.

"Alarm? Don't be stupid, Dant. I saw it fall into the ocean. A light like that, it is quite a sight even from a scroll." Bal sneers at Dant. Dant feels adrenaline building up inside him. He turns around and begins walking with heavy steps towards the distant Cymt. "What are you doing now?"

Bal starts to follow, quickly catching up to Dant's steady pace. Dant turns away from Bal again and walks towards the edge of the bridge. He stares down at the wild sea. The waves smash against one another with electric energy. Bal grabs Dant's shoulder and tries to pull him back to the vehicle. Before Dant knows what is happening, he has enclosed his hands around Bal's arm and pushes him with all his might. Dant backs away from the edge as Bal disappears from view. In the crashing of the waves, Dant does not hear the splash of his father's body against the water.

19
The S'chana Keepers
9/25/2499 5:45AM

Kidra wakes in the back of the large agricultural hauler. Its wide base allows for the transport of multiple myrlorx along secluded routes. Being at least one hundred years old, it requires substantial momentum before the batteries kick in for each of its seven wheels. Last night, Kidra had to assist in pushing it forward before scrambling to get onto its wide cargo bed. When it finally quickened, it made a noise, subito, like a gunshot. She had ducked down under the tarp, shaking with the memory of her father's assassination. The proximity sensor should have disabled all local firearms in the radius; Her father should have been safe. The s'chána keepers had deemed the malfunction a mystery and left it at that. Kidra considers the various security measures already accumulating across the land. If protocol is appropriately followed, all of the sensors will be disabled throughout Great Sular soon enough with the invading myrlorx.

She lies cramped between a score of myrlorx. She has noticed that all the myrlorx are fairly young, with the few older ones much more afflicted. She was shocked to learn just how large the myrlorx population has become. Not only do they surround the cities, but the population must be at least fifteen percent of that of Great Sular. Spying through a hole in the overspread tarp, she sees Isse still standing at the front of the vehicle, navigating with the emergency tristick.

Traveling at night helps, but it's always a risk, Isse had told her before the journey began. If they could avoid the authorities past the eastern forest, they would arrive at the eastern coast by seven o'clock. They would only arrive just in time for the third night's ceremony, but the myrlorx are hoping to catch the elders off guard. A small child to her right rouses with a yawn. Her new skin seems to be sitting well, overall, and should soon tighten completely. The child stands upright, balancing poorly on the moving vehicle. The wound to the back of her neck is barely visible now. Kidra had seen the child last night at the gathering. She had noticed that her siyalline skin was still loose and surmised that she must be the child from last night's ceremony.

"You should give her back. She is better off with them." Kidra had said to the myrlorx in response to the girl. The response was a loud guttural protest that became more and more intense. The myrlorx advanced and Kidra backed away. Isse had to put herself between them.

Kidra is shoved back with an elbow to her face as the hauler makes a tight turn. Kidra hears a sound from above. She looks up at the pink and blue sky. The clouds are finally parting after last night's rainfall.

"It's the s'chána keepers," Isse calls back from the front of the hauler. "I think they're doing a sweep of the woods." Kidra feels a sharp turn again and is rolled onto another myrlorx. The myrlorx responds with a sharp cry. Isse calls again, "Kidra, climb over here!"

Kidra looks at Isse who is frantically navigating against the tristick. Kidra climbs over the divider and squeezes into the small navigator box. The hauler's box is only designed for one person and Kidra is pressed uncomfortably between the glass and Isse.

"Kidra, we need to lay low, away from the woods, until the s'chána keepers retreat. We are not far from Hant." Isse thrusts the tristick to Kidra. "Take us somewhere safe."

"But if the s'chána keepers are going through the forest... Shouldn't we go back for--"

"Ghli will be fine. Do not worry about that."

Kidra is momentarily paralyzed with fear over Ghli. Ghli had remained with the other myrlorx in the safety of the forest. Kidra had been fearful of him becoming injured in the conflict. The myrlorx' plan is due to unfold tonight on the eastern coast. She had faith that the myrlorx would provide for Ghli deep in the woods. Despite his new appearance, Kidra had been so happy to see him eating heartily last night for the first time in years without the constraints of his taut skin. And already, he will soon be at the mercy of the authorities.

"They are going to the forests of South Ghi. The s'chána keepers do not venture that far. They've no need. Trust me, Kidra. Ghli will be safe," Isse says reassuringly. Kidra breathes out with relief. Her fears allay that Ghli will have to use the dagger she had left with him. It had been her inclination to keep him close that started this train of events to begin with. Since leaving, her desire to reach the eastern coast has only grown. She knows that she has to get to Dant as soon as possible.

The road before her is a familiar one. She pulls back on the tristick with her forearms. The heavy back of the hauler jostles upwards as the speed increases. The once busy roads are empty and quiet. Hant appears otherwise, eerily, the same. With one heavy turn after another, they arrive at the tall striped building. The purple color blends into the sky above and the gray stripes appear to divide the sky with a harsh finality. Kidra drives to the side of the building and pulls the tristick back.

"I don't think it will have enough momentum to drive up," Isse says, pointing towards the outstretched balconies high above. Kidra pushes the tristick downwards and the hauler's hum wanes. Kidra looks upwards again. "Do you have a vehicle pully up there?"

"Of course," Kidra replies. "There should be one accessible from the roof."

Isse frowns. "A communal one could be risky."

"Then we'll have to go elsewhere." Kidra raises the tristick again.

"No." Isse presses her hand down over Kidra's arm and the brief hum of the hauler is muted again. Isse looks towards the empty sky. "We need cover now." She turns to the cargo bed. "Out! We need to get up there!" Isse looks around before opening the door and exiting the hauler. She moves to the back and unlocks the cargo bed. The myrlorx spill out tentatively. Without their yellow cloaks, their stature is almost human-like. Without their silicone masks, Kidra's heart knew they couldn't be.

20
The Devil's Blood
9/25/2499 6:21AM

Rhode stirs with a heavy cough in her throat. The air has been left thick and dry from the fall. She raises her torso weakly, pushing her pulsating hands against the rough cave floor. In the harsh brightness, Teven is nowhere to be seen. A pool of small rocks spills down to Rhode's left side. She looks up to see Nal pushing her horn against the hole above. Soon a pile develops high enough onto which Nal can jump. She skids forward against the small rocks and lands next to Rhode. Rhode lets her head fall to Nal's. Through her closed eyes, she sees the intense brightness as she is enclosed by another memory.

Opening her eyes, she is surrounded by people. Cheers and jubilant screams come about around her. They face in one direction, but Rhode cannot see over the tall people to their site of focus. She feels her small body move forward, darting through gaps in the crowd. The wooden stage is brightly lit. A row of lights oscillates back and forth, causing her to stagger back, vertiginous. The man in the center of the stage raises his arms. His distinctive robes discern him as an elder, even in the obscurity of the rotating lights.

Another man on the stage thanks him, naming him as Elder Ish Tin. *Mr. Ish Tin!* In the highly contrasting hints of light, she can make out his face. It is unmistakably him. His voice rises and falls with the drums of the ceremony as he begins the familiar tale of The Devil's Blood. Rhode remembers the story instantly, though it has been many years since the last rendition. Rhode can recall the feeling of rebellion from eating the seeds of the puurron fruit that the children of Great Sular reveled in. Now the story seems different.

"The devil was a small man, with bright red skin and long black hair. He would torment God regularly, desperate to garner his time for his own. You see, the thing that he desired, or thought he desired, above all else was separateness from the Orthogonal Set. Their four thrones faced each other, representing the four cardinal directions. Each day, the devil would try to turn his throne around so as to look elsewhere from the six piercing eyes.

"At last, he came up with a deal. He traded his blood for his freedom from God. His blood was spilled onto the noble steps and under the feet of the cherished. With that, the land above became heaven to the Triumvirate of Arete. But little did the devil know that, without this blood, his movements would be weak, his voice faltering, and his thoughts buried beneath the smoldering flames that would crown his head. He crawled about the land, crying his empty laments. For years, he would drag his near limp body over fields, over mountains, over shallow marshes, nearly blinded by the harshness of the Sun. In the darkness, his eyes would soften and his body could rest in the serene boreal cold.

"But the devil was clever. And the devil was persistent. He found a weakly human in Illt. During her youth, she visited the forest every night. Unbeknownst to her, the devil began watching her wash her family's clothes in the lake. Eventually, he followed her everywhere she went. He cursed her food, piece by piece, until she could abide to eat nothing at all. She hungered greatly each day until she was near death. In her haggard state, the devil offered her the seed of a puurron fruit. He promised her that this seed was pure and untouched by poison or curse. In her desperation, she swallowed it. To her horror, the seed sprouted inside of her and the roots grew down her legs and the branches grew up to her head. Her blood was pushed to the outermost of her body and her skin became red and hot. She began bleeding from everywhere in her body and the devil took the blood for his own. The devil disappeared, his strength restored.

"Illt was shunned from her family and sought solace in a puurron tree. She ate only the seeds for the rest of her days. Every morning, she would bleed her red skin until it was as pale as snow, for her evil blood would replenish ten fold and two thousand times quicker than wholesome blood. After she married Trem, she kept this a secret, but she was soon enough discovered. The children of Trem and Illt became the devil's themselves as their children and their children's children eventually would. To separate them from us, is for our greater good. To please the Triumvirate of Arete and to be one with the divine, we offer a new skin."

Elder Ish Tin presents the ceremonial skin. The crowd cheers in a quiet collective with the same oblivious adulations as the festivals of Rhode's youth. Rhode recognises the siyalline skin as a model from thirty to forty years ago. Her own parents had worn such things. The pixel covers are larger, more easily differentiated from real skin than modern versions. A cry can be heard from the young child on stage and Rhode feels the urge to wince.

The ceremony closes, the lights dim, and the stage very slowly clears of its players. Rhode takes a good look at the emptying stage. The smoke above the flaming box reaches higher and higher towards the dark sky. The purple curtains around the stage rustle and then close from left to right. Rhode's eyes follow the movement until it reaches a brick wall. In front of it-- *Nal!* As clear as anything, Nal stands at the end of the stage. She twitches her face and disappears behind the closed curtain. Rhode forces the small body to walk forward towards the stage. Rhode has noticed that she is improving in the manipulation of the memory vessels during her travels. The body moves slowly, as if she is underwater, with the distinct force of gravity replaced by a wall of friction against her movements. She pulls the curtains over her and looks around. Robed elders congratulate one another and there is a collective relief in the air. She sees the main elder adjusting his robe fastening in a mirror. Rhode feels the body try to move away, but she holds firm. In the reflection of the mirror, she sees his face clearly. Mr. Ish Tin, some twenty years younger. And yet, so clearly Teven himself.

Rhode is pulled from the memory and is again in the large bright room, Nal to her side. She stands quickly, despite the pain in her body. She looks around frantically and rushes towards the only open tunnel in the room. She crawls through, this time agog to find the Elder Teven Ish Tin of years ago.

21
Jet
9/25/2499 7:01AM

Three elders from the northern regions surround Dant. Dant has received a great number of sympathies from the elders and remaining oracles regarding his father's death. Returning in the early hours of the morning, he had only to explain that Bal had fallen into the ocean due to the heavy storm. Dant's immediate return meant that the dialogues with Cymt will have to be postponed. No one had known that Bal was traveling up to meet them. Sulsu has said nothing since the incident. Dant had briefly considered sending her back to Hant, but judged it wise to keep her close. Dant, Sulsu, and two present oracles, Dolf and Whulè, are to remain here at least until the end of the light festival. They will be staying in the now complete tower, which sits tall, adjacent to the bridge's entrance way.

"As you have accepted the title, perhaps it would be best to begin your more rudimentary duties as Oracle, Dant," Whulè says, "Rather than waiting for the *festivities* to end." There is a silence in the room at the uncomfortable use of the term 'festivities'. The once joy-filled ceremonial arrangements now carry a sense of concrete foreboding.

"Indeed, with your father gone as well, the strength of the oracles will be perceived as faltering to say the least. You can at least participate in tonight's ceremony." Dolf shifts in his stance and draws his hands together in his wide sleeves. "The anticipation for Cymt dialogues will be heavily publicized. If all goes to plan."

"I would have handled the dialogues fine." Dant's voice falters in his reply. Dolf and Whulè look at one another. They had been reluctant for Dant himself to send word to Cymt of the need to postpone the dialogues, insisting that they will make the suitable arrangements in time.

"Sulsu should be present as well," Whulè adds. His expression sours before Dant's eyes.

Dant pauses before replying, "That won't be a problem."

The elders stare at Dant. Dant perceives that familiar look in their faces. The look that makes him believe he surely must have crawlers wriggling out of his ears, or else why would their eyes widen so?

"As a temporary measure," Dolf begins, "I propose asking my old friend Teven Ish Tin to fill in. He was a good worker before he retired. No need for you to take on the tasks of two oracles so soon." Dolf reaches out his hand and places it on Dant's shoulder.

Dant suppresses his anger at the confrontation of his own inadequacy. "We should make the announcement soon in that case."

"I will make the arrangements," Dolf offers. "You will need your rest, Dant."

Dant nods, turns to leave, but is stopped by Whulè.

"Shall I lead a prayer?" Whulè asks. The others bow their heads. "The light, the light. The future is light."

"Let light be us." The rest say collectively.

Dant lets a sneer escape his face as he turns quickly on the porcelain tiles below. His rapid footsteps echo through the wide room. Although the tower's design was created to inspire the confidence of the Cymt elders, such a size now seems crass to Dant. He knows little about Elder Nwirin Nnion of Cymt, but the Cymt people in general are known for their brutish characters.

Dant walks through the passageway to his bedroom, a small and dark room with far too much furniture already. As he opens the door, he sees Sulsu standing before him. He brushes past her, in no mood to converse further. As he does, he notices a musty smell indulating about the room. His eyes fall to a clear water jug with a distinctly black glow sitting on the thin shelf under the small slit of a window.

"Where did you get the ... *jet*?" Dant asks wearily.

Phosphorescent black light, or simply jet, as it is called in the central regions, is a drinkable form of trapped light. The light itself has been successfully marketed for its health properties, despite its offensive odor. It is the chemical nanosenic acid, that holds the light in suspension, which causes the acute intoxication that jet is known for.

"One should always have a source, should they not?" Sulsu stumbles slightly on her way to the window. Dant continues to stare vaguely in her direction. "I see how it is Dant. I do, really. You hate me, don't you?" Sulsu slinks onto a fainting couch in a relaxed position, draping her arms around the ornate gold plated raised back.

"It's not a matter of hate… per se." Dant begins a slow pace across the tiled floors.

"I don't know what else you want from me. I'm here, aren't I? I've said nothing, haven't I? Nothing about so much now." Sulsu takes a large sip from her jug of jet before pouring a section into a glass. "That's much better. Anyway, I'm used to this already. 'Specially after living with *them* for that long. *Too* long. I don't want to go back to Ji." With every sip, more of her original dialect is slipping through, in a grotesque hybrid of Hant and Ji.

Dant looks through the window. The sea seems almost frozen in its stillness. "It's a shame you feel that way. I may have to send you back soon."

"I doubt that. Somehow." Sulsu smiles at Dant and reaches her hand out to him "Dant, come. We used to be *good* friends, didn' we? Why it was only a day ago that y' embraced me as your wife." Dant holds his hand out and feels Sulsu's gentle squeeze. "It's n' my fault you're sloppy 'n your crimes. And I don' just mean with *your* father." Dant's thoughts drift back to the assassination of Kidra's father. He remembers her scream when Oracle Daller Pi collapsed. "'Ave you seen this?" Sulsu pushes her scroll at Dant.

Dant blinks at the bright screen. A reporter speaks to her colleague and an image appears centrally, growing to fill the whole scroll. The image shows the multiple blood stains on the walls of his apartment.

"... of evidence of a break-in in the apartment of newly appointed Oracle Dant Pi Tel and the late Kidra Pi Tel. Our sources confirm that Oracle Pi Tel remains on the East Coast. It is speculated that the break in and subsequent attack took place during the first night of light. The s'chana keepers are awaiting aDNA and rDNA results from the labs but drop tests suggest that the blood belongs to Ghli Pi Tel. It is all but certain that the myrlorx are behind the incident."

Dant sighs. Ghli is always an afterthought. An image of Kidra smiling on the cover a local magazine issue appears on the screen.

"Kidra Pi Tel was a beloved member of Great Sular Oracle society. Daughter of renowned scholar Oracle Daller Pi, Kidra rose to fame after her wedding to Dant Tel. Since then, she inspired thousands with her elegance and poise during the ceremonies of Great Sular. During the pre-ceremony line up tonight, tune in to see the life of Kidra

Pi Tel in detail as we share highlights in the commemorative special at six."

Sulsu pulls the scroll back and rolls it up.

"They don't seem to like *me* though. Genuinely. N' even a mention. Kidra's still Miss Popular. Isn't that interesting?" Sulsu gulps down the remaining jet in her glass as the glass dims. She allows it to drop to the floor where it cracks in four clean pieces. Dant's upper lip twitches.

"Yes," Dant replies with biting sarcasm. "Isn't it just. Just so *terribly, terribly* interesting."

"Well, you can't be angry about that. You killed her, didn't you?" Sulsu asks rhetorically as Dant closes his eyes. "It's true, Dant. I've never been one for fear or such nonsense. And why not have fun and intrigue while we can." Dant opens the door and leaves. Sulsu's voice follows him down the hallway. "You're still Mr. Popular. You haven't damaged that *yet*."

Dant feels his body convulse. His spy has assured him that Kidra is still alive. It is only a matter of time. Footsteps approach. Dant remains still. Off the corner, he sees the shadows of Dolf and Whulè.

"The power grid continues to waver."

"The myrlorx?"

"No! Well. It is unlikely. This is coming from deeper than they can get to. Possibly the tunnels."

Dant feels his index finger tap against his thigh. *That machine in Fhi!*

"Yes, I wouldn't think the myrlorx would be much of a threat to that."

"But we need to get ahead of it, in any case. It has drained the power systems in the west and is due to reach Hant this morning."

"In that case, if we want the ceremony to be broadcast without interruption, the only alternative I can think of is to create a new power grid."

"Ah, expenses, expenses."

22
The Past
9/25/2499 7:31AM

Puddles drench the entirety of the balcony. Wet footsteps are visible on the inner carpet. Kidra had been shocked at the sight of the blood covering the walls, the floor, when they had opened the front door. Her first thought was Ghli, but he is still safe in the woods. *What could have happened?* S'chana keeper's tape section off the majority of the room. Small plastic gloves have been haphazardly left about the floor.

Isse had put her hand on Kidra's shoulder. "The s'chana keepers will likely be back at some point." Isse had said. "We should get some supplies and go."

The myrlorx are still rummaging through the apartment, taking what they judge to be of use. Kidra looks away, walks to her bedroom. She pushes the door open with her elbow and looks around at the grandeur of all of her belongings. Two long screens stand on either side of the long window. The opulent carvings of wood around the black screens extend down to a long dresser connecting them. Kidra sees her clothing, and outfit for the first night's ceremony, flung on the green velvet chair in the corner of the room. A pair of elbow length golden gloves sit on top. She looks down at what little is left of hands.

Kidra sits down on a soft stool in front of the right screen. She uses her wrist to activate the touch screen. An enlarged mirrored image of herself appears before her. The dried blood of the myrlorx appears pasted to her face. She sees her face pale in the uneasiness. The blood transfusion that she had received had been from Ghli. Kidra feels briefly sickened by the thought of Ghli's increasingly bright skin. A sense of shame creeps in that she could feel like this about him. She remembers his hollowed face after the surgery. She imagines the inflammation and necrosis that must have been occurring behind his eyes that resulted in the amputations; His body forcing out pieces of the microchips in large black tumors under his eyelids, pressing them out.

Following the gathering, Ghli had asked Kidra if she had known that the allotting children are stolen from the myrlorx. "Yes, I did know, Ghli," Kidra had admitted. The myrlorx children are always taken young enough that they can adapt. Kidra shudders at the thought of the myrlorx raising the infant version of Ghli and the fate of her son should he remain with them, banished into perversion.

She wipes the blood from her face away with her sleeve, feeling the wetness of fresh tears in her eyes. She pushes open a small makeup box with difficulty. In trying to raise a brush with her two wrists, she drops it onto the surface of the dresser. It falls with a bang onto another and rolls off onto the floor.

"You look like you're getting ready for a party." Isse says from the doorway.

Kidra pushes the make up to one side with her wrists.

"Oh, I didn't mean anything by it." Isse walks over, picks up the brush from the floor, and looks at Kidra's face on the screen. "Let me help you."

"Oh, It's hardly necessary."

"Well, now. We want to make an impression on the elders, I'm sure." Isse picks up a palette from the dresser, opening it with one hand. She taps the tip of the brush into a circle of color and applies the soft eyeshadow to Kidra's closed eyelids. Kidra feels the soft brush against her skin and below her eyelashes.

"What are you doing with *them*?" Kidra whispers. Isse stops for a moment before replying.

"We are our circumstances. That is our destiny."

Kidra thinks back to the child from the ceremony and shudders. Suddenly, something occurs to Kidra. "But your accent--"

"Now, what color would you like?" Isse holds up a palette of three lipstick shades.

"I usually use the red one, but I'm not sure now."

Isse dips the brush into the pale pink liquid and delicately paints over Kidra's bottom lip. "Lovely." Kidra looks back at her reflection in the dim screen.

Suddenly, the image flickers and the screen shuts off with a short trill. Isse looks up and whispers, "Power outage." She walks quickly to the bedroom door and looks back to say, "Don't be too long now. We should be moving soon."

Kidra looks back at her reflection in the dim black screen and quickly stands. She considers what going home publicly will mean. The elders will never concede that Ghli is a creature as this would impact the natural order of the oracles. Kidra herself will have no one to vouch for her whereas Dant's slight favor with the bridge construction very well may be impactful. In any case, a war is inevitable. Kidra makes her way back to the lounge of the apartment. The sound of the myrlorx rustling through her belongings has curiously quietened. As she turns the last corner, she sees why.

Bal is standing in the entrance way of the apartment waving a firearm in the direction of the myrlorx. Kidra immediately tenses. The proximity sensors that protect the building will be down in the power outage. Bal walks further into the apartment, towards Isse. A look of confusion spreads over his face.

"Bal," Kidra says loudly. "Put the gun down."

Bal turns to Kidra with a distorted expression on his face. "What are you doing here? Alive. With them." He growls, holding his gun towards her.

"I can explain if you would, please..."

"Is Ghli here too, then?" Bal walks closer to her now. "Have you joined up with those things, then? Trust Dant to raise one and marry one."

Kidra feels her heart pounding in her chest. Her eyes focus on the barrel of the gun and Bals finger twitching over the trigger. Suddenly he falls to the floor with a shattering of glass and wilted flowers. Isse stands over him, her eyes wide. Kidra quickly reaches for the gun as Bal grunts. Kidra looks up to Isse and sees behind her a landed rotelcopter on the balcony with several s'chana keepers on their way.

23
Redemption
9/25/2499 8:41AM

Teven races through the tunnel, pulling his body across the limestone walls, wriggling in a ghostlike swiftness. *How could this be true?* He had seen the memory with Rhode. His mission had seemed so clear when Mr. Ish Tin had explained it to him. *Mr. Ish Tin. Me.*

In the inn, Mr. Ish Tin had told Teven about his life as an elder. About his work. And his passion. And importantly, his future. Teven was told many reasons why the tunnels of time are obstructed to Mr. Ish Tin. Now that his joints are ossified and arteries calcified, the act of contorting his body within the caves would be a tortuous endeavor. But before age had whittled him away, Mr. Ish Tin had told him, he had seen what will become of this world. He had told Teven what he had seen and it put shivers down Teven's spine. The crux of it will be Rhode. That much is clear. And that is why Teven must stop her now. Or in any time that he can within the caves, before future events unfold.

And how many times has he been convinced to complete this mission? Before his arrival to the inn, he had heard the baby cry, while in another memory. It was *her*. It was *Rhode*. Born primitively in society like some juxtaposition of nature. Mr. Ish Tin would he had killed her then. A perception of remorse filters into Teven's mind. It seemed so easy then. She had seemed so purely malicious when Mr. Ish Tin had eludicated the events. But in the memories he had seen, her actions thus far indicate no malfeasance. Indeed, in his travels this time, the memories have served *only* to heighten his curiosity in regards to the creatures and how they came about. *Mr. Ish Tin knows more than he implied. That much is certain.*

But now he knows he *is* Mr. Ish Tin. Is he himself merely a past ghostly concoction or something else entirely? *I need to find another memory.* Teven has grown to feel at home within the darkness of the tunnels. The calm silence in the tunnels and the endless knowledge in the memories are an entire world of possibilities. And the twisting overlapping maze of tunnels have a way of leading one just where they need to go. He stops and listens. Listens for echoes of movement. He feels upwards a gap in the tunnel and pulls himself to the opening. Forward now, he sees the glistening light of another room of stalagmites. Footsteps. Teven crawls forward through the widening tunnel. He closes his eyes when he reaches the room, allowing his pupils to constrict. When he opens them again, he sees her. Rhode is staring into a small pool of water, her reflection rippling violently.

"That might prove dangerous," Teven says. Rhode does not look away. Teven moves behind her and looks into the moving water. Her distorted reflection comes and goes in pieces. "What do you see?"

"Myself," she replies. "Just flickers. In different times." Rhode visibly shakes. "Like some pitiful ... ragged myrlorx, drowning in its own poverty." Her shaking increases further. She does not break her gaze. Teven hesitates before pulling her away from the water, his arms wrapped around her. She gasps at the release of the image.

"You need to be careful of the water here. There are things that can't be unseen." Teven looks at Rhode, whose eyes begin to widen as she looks into his. "I'm sorry," he whispers. He explains to Rhode that Mr. Ish Tin had convinced him to enact his plan, that somehow he and Mr. Ish Tin are one and the same, and that he is sick with guilt over his part in this. "It will happen. Because of you. In six months from now. You'll do it. And it will be over."

"What is it that happens?" Rhode asks, trying to stop her gaze from finding its way back to the glistening water.

Teven frowns. "Perhaps it does not happen anyway, not anymore." He moves to the tunnel walks, feeling the edges with his fingers. "We should get out of here. Time moves differently here. Time can speed up or slow down or move as it should. We just can't know how long we've been here already."

"How? How will we get out?"

"I'll show you. Follow me." Teven holds his hand to Rhode, urging her to stand up.

Rhode looks up at him and then back to the tunnel she had crawled through. "But Nal. She'll be trapped."

"Trapped? A solceros? They evolved in caves like this. A manifestation of the shared consciousness. Solceros can come and go as they please."

Rhode's eyebrow raises slightly.

"For us the portal is limited. Let's just hope the light festival is still going on. Otherwise it will be ... tricky."

Rhode stands, looks down, and then nods.

Teven pauses as the realization sinks in that he really will be leaving the caves. He feels more at home here than anywhere else. And in the deep of the memories, the tunnels overshadow any hint of his own. He closes his eyes and then they go.

24

The Return
9/25/2499 1:14PM

Tears well up in Dant's eyes at the sight of Kidra. His mouth gapes open with shock at his own emotion, shock that he could have thought that he held only disdain for her. He presses his tongue onto the floor of his mouth, to hold back words of love. He breathes in hard in an attempt to hold the rest inside too. Kidra, her arms gilded in long golden gloves, walks into the large room of the makeshift temple-like entrance way of the tower. Her stained and soiled dress clings tightly to her shape. A s'chana keeper stands on either side of her. Behind them, two other figures appear as shadows in the immense open metal doors. Kidra reaches down to her ankle. In an instant, Isse is by her side, straightening her torso. Isse stills abruptly when she sees Dant's expression. Dant presses his fingers into the arms of his wingback chair. He motions to Isse to come closer still before looking to Kidra again.

"Happily ever after. How could it have ever seemed real?" Dant mutters to himself.

"I never thought it could be anyway." Kidra looks behind Dant shoulder to Isse now standing next to a s'chana keeper. "Don't you know where Ghli is right now?"

"Things like that are of no consequence to me. They *can't* be," he whispers to her, silently urging her to her own silence in the presence of the oracles. Dant whispers to Isse and Whulè leads her to another room. Dant looks back to the door and sees the remaining shadow has gone. He stands. "Come, Kidra."

Dant and Kidra walk down a set of stairs, through a multitude of underground corridors. They pass many rooms, primitively constructed and unfurnished. The sound of their footsteps is interrupted only by the heavy panting of a myrlorx in one room, confined. As they walk side by side, Dant steals glances at Kidra. Her eyes remain forward and her pace is steady, as if she had lived in this new construction all her life. Dant can now hear the loud whispers of Dolf and Whulè, who are walking behind them. Dant grimaces at their distinct hissings.

"Another machine in Central Sular?"

"This is getting ridiculous."

"Do not pay them attention, that will only garner interest in it from the people."

"Time crawling will only become more prominent if this keeps up. And then it's only a matter of time before people get curious about the origins of the myrlorx."

"Preposterous!"

At last they reach the end of the final corridor. Dant walks up to the black wall. The darkness blends into his hair and deep blue robe. He presses his hand to the wall and a hidden door slides open.

"Welcome," he says through gritted teeth and enters the room. Kidra stands in the entrance way, staring at the stark features of the room. "You'll be safe here. If that's what you want."

Dolf and Whulè are suddenly behind Kidra and they usher her into the room. Dant's smirks at this and moves to the doorway again.

"Sulsu and I live upstairs ... of course." Dant allows his gaze to linger on Kidra for a moment before stepping out of the room and allowing the door to slide closed. After stomping in place for a moment, he leans back and turns his head to his right. He allows his breathing to quiet such that he can hear Dolf's pompous chuckles.

"It was by chance that the s'chana keepers found you. Thank heavens they did. No, don't tell us the details."

Whulè speaks more gruffly. "We trust you will rest well here." He clears his throat. "Here. Read this."

After a few minutes, he can hear Kidra saying something, but cannot make out what.

"The letter is quite clearly from Ghli," Dolf states. "Based on the content, he must have written it perhaps two, three hours past."

"The s'chana keepers intercepted it before it could arrive on your scroll," Whulè explains. "Not that you would have seen it."

"We do apologize, Kidra. The s'chana keepers will replace your scroll soon enough. And it's nothing urgent, is it? From the sound of it, Ghli is starting to become more confident and eating well."

"I doubt that he should come here though."

"Don't let Whulè worry you, Kidra. No, it certainly won't do to have him here ... or any of your myrlorx friends."

Dant hears Kidra again, louder than before, but her words remain muffled.

"Just stay here for now Kidra. I'm sure we can put together a public statement to explain your whereabouts in a more palatable way. The public will be positively exultant."

Dant walks forward now, hurriedly through the corridor and up the stairwell. The presentiment of the ceremony and the obscurity of the future charge his legs with a frenzy of energy.

25
Mr. Ish Tin
9/25/2499 3:00PM

Mr. Ish Tin stands in front of the screen wall. He turns to his side, twisting his head to consider his reflection. It had been a great many years since he had donned his elders robes. The darker oracle robes that he dons now are comparable, but certainly provide an illustrious aura that had been missing in the days of his eldership. *Tonight's ceremony will be spectacular.* His retirement as an elder had been premature in his eyes, though 'necessary' according to his colleagues due to his preoccupation with time travel.

"Papa," Mitya calls from downstairs. "Were ye expectin' t'guests back wut from las' yesderday?"

Mr. Ish Tin straightens his posture and walks over to the window. Below him, he sees a fading green glow from the machine and beside it, Teven and Rhode. "*Not* again," he mutters to himself. "Surely I was never so naive." He makes his way down the creaking stairs and out to the humidity of the afternoon's Sun. He feels an eerie foreboding in the empty streets. In the one story house across the street he sees a curtain being closed quickly. *Another attack here is unlikely,* he tries to convince himself. Despite himself, he feels the strong desire to get back to security behind a closed door. "Help me Mitya!" He points at the two unconscious bodies on the ground. Mitya potters over and cautiously pokes her head out into the fresh air. She looks down and shakes her head. Together, they carry the two one by one onto the living room floor. Mitya pushes the front door closed with a bang and turns both the middle and the bottom locks. The sound seems to cause Rhode to stir.

Rhode grabs hold of her head with both hands before opening her eyes. Mr. Ish Tin sends Mitya to the back of the house to check on Machova. Once Mitya has left the room, Mr. Ish Tin puts his hand on Rhode's shoulder.

"There, there, young lady. You must have had quite a time in those caves." He stands and offers her his hand. Rhode takes it and is pulled up to a standing position. She wobbles noticeably and places her hands back onto her head only briefly. She reaches around for something to steady herself. Mr. Ish Tin pulls a chair out to the middle of the room and helps her to take a seat. "Now I suppose you remember little at present."

"No. I'm sorry," Rhode stammers. "Where am I?"

"You'll remember soon enough." Mr. Ish Tin walks towards the kitchen. "Excuse me for a moment." Mr. Ish Tin returns with warm bubbling lohqra liquid, finding Rhode staring worriedly at Teven's unconscious body. "He'll be fine soon enough. Motion sickness from the travels. As you have too. Here. Drink this."

Mr. Ish Tin sits down across the table from Rhode. Rhode sips the liquid slowly, pausing often to push her hand against her forehead. Mr. Ish Tin smiles, nodding at each sip. Suddenly, Rhode stops. She stares hard at Mr. Ish Tin. Her eyes widen. Mr. Ish Tin's smile grows. She stands with great difficulty and hobbles to the door. She drapes her body against it and unlocks one, then two locks. She tugs at the door and then surrenders to gravity, collapsing in a pile on the floor.

"I'm afraid it's dangerous out there. You won't remember yet, but the myrlorx invaded the first night of light." Mr. Ish Tin sits back, letting the back of his head touch the window frame, admiring the way his robe sleeve shimmers in the light. Rhode looks at the empty glass on the table. "In my youth, I had been regrettably sympathetic towards them. It's times like these that I regret so much of what I did." His eyes meet Rhode's. "But it's never too late to make things right." He raises himself and walks towards Rhode. "You were born here, you know, before your parents claimed you. I know.

Disgusting, isn't it?" He sees her eyes struggling to stay focussed as she stares up at him. "But that's how benign my actions were towards their kind. They would take refuge here in such vulnerable times." He places the front of his boot against Rhode's head. "Now let's get you back to the tunnels. Let you die elsewhere." He presses his foot against her again, confident that she is sufficiently numbed.

Mr. Ish Tin unlocks the bottom bolt on the door and pushes Rhode back outside, next to the machine. He exhales loudly and sets the pedals forward. Coming back in through the open door, he looks down at Teven's still body. He grimaces as he begins dragging the body up the stairs. He finds each step a great difficulty and considers calling for Mitya's help again, but he knew she was too simple to understand such matters. He thinks for a moment that he can see Teven's left eye flicker as he reaches the top step.

Now breathing deeply, Mr. Ish Tin pulls Teven's body to the window. He lets it fall to the floor as he fiddles with the lock on the window. The key is stuck again. He lets out an expletive and tries again. At last the window is open. He feels first the cool breeze and then the familiar heat from the Sun. All of a sudden, he feels a hard pressure on the back of his head. He turns around and sees Teven upright and towering over him. Mr. Ish Tin steps back and loses his balance. As he quakes, Teven thrusts his arms forward.

Teven sees a flash of green as Mr. Ish Tin disappears from view. Teven leans forward and pushes his hands into his thighs. *What have I done? But what choice did I have?* He rushes downstairs through the open door to find Rhode. In her weak state, she crawled into the doorway and escaped the portal's light. Teven helps her inside and sits her up against the wall.

"I'm sorry." Teven says. "I didn't know what he... or *I*... was going to do. I pretended to be out of it." Teven puts his hand to his forehead. "Not that my head isn't pounding."

"Then you heard; I'm as good as a myrlorx," Rhode whispers. "Born from myrlorx, raised by nomadic sympathizers." Rhode looks into Teven's eyes. "No matter what you go through, you'll never truly understand loneliness."

"And you do, I take it."

"Again and again, with every breath I take."

They are interrupted by footsteps over the creaking floors behind Teven. He turns quickly to see Machova come bouncing into the room. Teven smiles as the dog barks at the window. Rhode turns to see a much larger Nal knocking her horn against the glass.

"But for her. She's a real solceros now."

Teven looks at her for a moment, as the tears fall from Rhode's cheeks, and then reaches for her hands. "Wait for the s'chana keepers." Rhode looks back to Teven and sharply inhales as he seems to disappear into thin air.

26
Kidra

9/25/2499 6:06PM

Kidra watches her face move across the screen wall of the small room from the hard bed. Her death has been highly publicized. Kidra scoffs at the overzealousness of it all. She opens the scroll that Dolf had left for her and rereads Ghli's letter. Ghli had been shown a news story in relation to Dant. Ghli is adamant in his letter that he cannot stand to leave her with Dant. *And I cannot stand to leave you with* them. She hears the doors slide open behind her. She doesn't recognise the young girl but knows her instantly.

Sulsu enters with forced grace. "If we could skip the pleasantries." She forces a quick smile and sits on the small bed next to Kidra. "Do you intend to stay?" Sulsu looks around the room as if disgusted.

Kidra considers this, "I suppose I do. Where else can I go?"

"You've been gone too long. You don't know the first thing about what we've been through in the last three days. The attack changed everything."

"Yes, it certainly did. Why wouldn't I understand that?"

Sulsu frowns. "The ceremony cannot go ahead, you know. That old Oracle who was supposed to fill in for Bal has vanished. He did not show up to the rehearsal. The s'chana keepers were called to Fhi about an hour ago to investigate."

"For Bal?" Kidra asks, confused.

Sulsu rolls her eyes. "See? It's too much for you. There was a bright light apparently. And someone was there. Some girl from Cymt. Well, Cymtian by relegation."

Kidra tilts her head to one side.

"They brought her in for questioning. S'chana keepers have become a delivery service. Is this the kind of government you wish to be a part of? *I* can make a difference 'ere. What's the point of living with these bodies and minds if we are to be mindless robots? We might as well be like *them* and pull out the microchips, the metal in our bones, if we can't use our spines!" Sulsu collapses onto the bed in tears. Kidra places a hand gently on Sulsu's back. "I hate him!" Sulsu spits. "How did you stand him? He's nothing like they show he is!"

Kidra ponders the question. "It didn't really come up," Kidra answers. "He and I were told we were to be together, so we were. Tolerating one another didn't really play a part."

The glow of the screen flashes more brightly. Kidra and Sulsu look at the screen. A line at the bottom of the screen flashes the words Breaking News.

"A victory for the citizens of Great Sular. The brave s'chana keepers of the central regions have located a large gathering of myrlorx in the forests of South Gli." Kidra's eyes widen as drone footage shows a sweep view of tall trees with the unmistakable white flowers of South Gli. "It is believed that this group is responsible for the attack on Fhi, the first city, on the night of the first ceremony of light. A night that has since spurned fear among the people of Great Sular."

"Don't get too excited. From what I hear, they only found a single dead myrlorx. The rest fled, got away." Sulsu rolls her eyes, her tears dry.

Kidra looks at Sulsu and is revolted by the blasé disconnect between the official communique and what is true in this world; The nonchalant falsehood that she herself had presented all her life, that she had been so proud of, now falls to disgrace.

The commentator continues, "It is unclear whether or not restrictions will be lifted following tonight's ceremony. Perhaps with the closure, the people of Great Sular can move forward from this unprecedented event and look towards the future with the arrival of the Elder Nwirin Nnion of Cymt in coming days to begin the long awaited dialogues with newly appointed Oracle Dant Pi Tel."

The drone footage lowers to the ground towards a mound of dirt with an array of flowers. As the image appears closer still, Kidra realized that the mound is a dead myrlorx. She gasps when it hits her; It is Ghli. Her body begins to shake and she feels her chest suppress a cry. She rises from the bed and tries to slide the door open. Ignoring the biometric lock, she begins pulling at the door harder and harder until she is banging on the sides in a frenzy. Sulsu silently presses her finger to the lock and pulls it away quickly as Kidra rushes through.

As she runs through the corridors, Kidra hears the rapid thuds of her footsteps, or her heartbeat, or both, like drums banging loudly within her ears. *Ghli is dead.* Images flash through her mind. The myrlorx surrounding him and stabbing him. *The dagger I gave him.* The s'chana keepers shooting him from afar. *I made him stay.* His muted cries, alone in the woods, never having learned to call out with the guttural cries of the other myrlorx. *The* other *myrlorx.*

Kidra reaches the entrance way of the tower and pushes past the two s'chana keepers on either side of the wide doorway. She absent mindedly throws herself onto the ground. She feels herself pushing away the grass, pushing her gloves stumps into the earth. The moist air and the cold wet soil that leech through her gloves are somehow comforting. Small roots protrude from the earth and scratch against her. She imagines herself crawling around him, burying Ghli deep in the ground.

27
Emptiness
9/25/2499 6:39PM

Rhode walks towards the large entrance way of the great tower. The cool wind has increased even since she was taken off the rotelcopter. The s'chana keeper who is gripping her arm is speaking to an unknown voice through his earpiece. Rhode can make out a deepness to the faraway voice, but is unable to discern its content. Since the s'chana keepers' arrival at the inn, the s'chana keepers had had difficulty in choosing a course of action. It was clear that they were being given conflicting orders. Rhode had explained that Mr. Ish Tin's younger self Teven had revealed himself as a hologram, disappearing after he had pushed Mr. Ish Tin into the open portal to the time tunnels. The s'chana keepers were comically careful not to go near the inactive machine. Now, she gathered, she was being taken either to tell the events to the elders in person or to be taken directly back to Cymt. She had began shaking in the rotelcopter at the sight of the bridge though was comforted by the approaching ground as they landed at the tower. As they walk across the uneven grass, she sees the large tent, with small specks hovering around it: The studio and cameras in preparation for the ceremony tonight. She had learnt that it was true that following the attack, the rest of the ceremonies are closed to live viewings. She breathed another sigh of relief that she had not been lost within the tunnels for too long. She and Teven had escaped the caves by jumping from a great distance. This proved difficult to find in the darkness, but Teven eventually found a memory stream beaming off a cliff. Now Teven is gone, the hologrammed version of a young Mr. Ish Tin searching in the ethers for a purpose. The creation of holograms was a controversial matter. With usually only a simple task in mind, such as relaying information in real time, rogue versions can develop the ability to learn, to reason, to react. When found, they are so often destroyed. If Mr. Ish Tin created Teven, then surely Teven is saved from such a fate at least. In the commotion of the s'chana keepers arrival, Nal had run off. She has become quicker still, gone from view in a mere instant.

Two figures walk towards the tent behind Rhode. "The power will be sufficient for the ceremony. Quite a decent surge came through this afternoon," One says. Neither of the elder robed men give a second look to Rhode or the s'chana keeper at her arm.

They reach the entrance way to the tall tower. Rhode is in awe of the immensity of the room. Her small footsteps echo loudly against the ceiling far above. She looks to the s'chana keeper who looks around, as if frightened by the emptiness of the room.

"Tiitch enso!" *The s'chana keepers' command.* The voice comes from outside, possibly from one of the elders. The s'chana keeper drops Rhode, having been holding her so tightly and so high. She falls to the hard marble floor, feeling the vibrations of the s'chana keeper's heavy footsteps. She looks back towards the entrance way to see that the s'chana keeper had already disappeared to his mission. Uncertain, she gathers herself and exits the tower. She hears the s'chana keepers running. Following the sounds, she finds herself gazing upon the immense structure of the bridge. The metal surface appears to go on forever and is a welcome obstruction of the view of Cymt. She sees no s'chana keepers on the bridge, the vast emptiness of it full with reflected light. She thinks it almost pretty, but for its purpose. The road to Cymt is here, her return is imminent, more straightforward than before. She collapses to the ground, wishing to be back in the caves, in the safety of the shielding darkness.

28
The Children
9/25/2499 7:05PM

Dant feels all of his fears fall away as the ceremony begins. It is remarkable. At last he has found his feet, leading the ceremony as a true oracle. His sleep deprived body almost vibrates with excitement. Dolf hands him the flame and Dant alights the torch while Whulè looks on, nodding at each of Dant's carefully choreographed motions. The small cameras rotate around him quickly, building a three dimensional image to be projected on the screens of all in Great Sular. Dant clears his throat but Dolf shakes his head gently. He stands in front of Dant and asks "Shall we begin?" to the darting cameras. He steps onto the box and opens the book.

"The Story of The Children of The Myrlorx. Trem's genes were forever tainted because of his association with Illt. Though he banished the children of Illt, the first myrlorx were a clever bunch, as the devil lives within their thickened blood.

"Trem's second wife Muuila came upon a baby in the forest. The child was seen as a gift from god itself, for the trees around the baby were red with the Sun's fire. Trem was overjoyed, for he would have an heir.

"Day after day, Muuila would play with the child, teach it the ways of the true. Until one day, after several years, Muuila noticed a peculiarity in the child. He did not seem to grow like other children. Neigh, he stood short in stature. And when he was watched, he seemed poorly and lilt, while others would tell Muuila that he danced with exuberance when she was looking away.

"It was clear to all that the young child, in his infancy, was swapped with a myrlorx child. Trem took action and destroyed the beast.

"Trem ordered that no children may only be chosen from the forest before their liminal age ..."

Dant maintains a soft expression with force. The many flames within the tent create a high contrast to the edges of the elders' faces. The wind pulls at the door flap of the tent and Dant can see it is now unmanned. *Where had the s'chana keepers run off to?*

Dant watches Dolf, with a smile pressed into his face. *He's just a rotting corpse of a man spewing nonsense in a tent with insects gathering around the mounds of dug up soil. And what am I?*

Suddenly, he sees the cameras retreat, one by one, as if activated by their motion sensors. He glances at Whulè, whose expression of consternation is more pronounced than usual. He follows Whulè's gaze and almost does a double take. *What is she doing now?*

29
Iníon
9/25/2499 7:01PM

Kidra sees the girl's small frame, collapsed on the entrance of the bridge. The girl's gaze appears to be unable to break from the great structure. Kidra is overcome with the image of Ghli, his fragile shell collapsed into darkness. Her arms stretch and wrap around the girl. She draws her close, feeling the possession pacify her despair. The girl looks up at her and wipes her tears from below her eyes. Kidra recognises the girl's dress as one belonging to an emigrant of the Mass Relegation.

"What's wrong?" Kidra asks. Rhode doesn't answer. Kidra stands, prompting Rhode to rise. "Are you the one to do with the elder's disappearance?"

Rhode nods. "I recognise you," she says, pondering how. *The Pi Tels, yes... but something about that look.* "I saw you. In the tunnels." Rhode closes her eyes and pictures the memory. "You called to me, as someone else. From a lavish garden party. I waited by the pond." She brings her hands up to her cheeks, "And what pain!" She opens her eyes to see Kidra's confused expression. Rhode explains her rudimentary understanding of the tunnels and the glimpses of memories they allow.

Kidra's face falls. "That must have been Ghli's pain. My son." Kidra feels light headed with her knees threatening to buckle. Now Rhode holds Kidra by the arms, giving her enough leverage to remain standing. "It *is* my fault," Kidra whispers. She turns to the tent, its walls glowing with the ceremonial flames. "There are things I know. I shouldn't have kept it all back like this." She looks up to the blinking Sun, that glaring evidence of humanity's failed attempt at the Dyson sphere. Kidra stands and walks towards the tent.

30
Crash
9/25/2499 7:20PM

Dant sees her shadow as she approaches the tent. The motion sensors of the cameras, too, react and move subtly towards the doorway. The flap of the tent opens. She looks directly at him, with that superior look. *What a fool I was to weep at her return!*

Dant feels a jolt of energy, excited that if she should attack, he can release himself at last. But then his body wilts from within. He knows how these events will play out; He can see the resolve on her face. And it does. She makes some loud claim, accusation. Dant knows it is over. Over the live broadcast, the public now know she is alive. That is all it will take for him to lose it all. Dant is doomed to fall out of favor. *You wanted this, Kidra! It was you who wanted this fame. Well, you'll get it.*

A crashing sound can be heard from the bridge. An elder rushes out of the tent. Dolf quickly shuts off the cameras with his scroll and they drop to the ground one by one. Another sound, louder. Dant walks out of the tent with the other elders. Towards the bridge, he sees the s'chana keepers coming up from the underside side of the bridge. The oracles step out of the tower one by one. Confused, he looks around. Before he has a chance to turn, a large group of myrlorx rush past him from behind the tent. The loud sound and rushing bodies leave Dant in a momentary stupor. Then the stench hits him. There must be a few hundred of them. The group run towards the bridge. Kidra looks out of the tent, her arm covering her mouth. Dolf smiles gently.

The myrlorx and the s'chana keepers meet head on. The s'chana keepers delay in their attack. *Use your firearms, you idiots.* The s'chana keepers appear to be herding the myrlorx back towards the tower, slowing their pace. The oracles advance towards them. Spreading out, they arrange themselves in a circle around the myrlorx. Each oracle removes a small bag of powder from their pocket and lets it escape in the air.

Dolf nudges Kidra and explains, "Carbon monoxide." Dant watches as the myrlorx collapse, some fall still while others continue writhing in the ground. Dolf clasps his hands behind his back, proudly looking on. "Despite their seemingly increased blood flow, it is in fact only to the interstitial fluid. Their circulating oxygen is quite low, leaving them more vulnerable to atmospheric changes than you or I."

Dant sees Kidra's face falls into disappointment. Despite himself, he feels it too. That the myrlorx were defeated so easily means the relentless continuation of the status quo. The s'chana keepers drag the myrlorx bodies into a netting. A rotelcopter lowers from the sky and carries the netting west.

31
Réamhfhocal
9/25/2499 8:59PM

Kidra leads Rhode to her room in the tower, having been issued Dant's former room by the elders. Dant's arrest was immediate after the s'chana keepers returned. When Bal had arrived to speak against Dant, claiming that Dant had attempted to kill him, Dant was left speechless. Evidently, Dant had mistaken Bal's hologram, which Bal had controlled remotely from Hant, for his real father. The power surges following this had left Bal unable to inform the elders of this until now. Kidra remembers Dant's face as his hands were bound by the s'chana keepers. Half of his eyes had disappeared under his heavy eyelids. The corners of his mouth curled slightly. He seemed to personify relief more than anything else. She had approached him before the s'chana keepers took him to the lower dungeons of the tower. She had wanted to say something cruel to him, something to expel the alleviation from him. But instead, in a lowered whisper, she asked him of the myrlorx; She asked of their origins, of some piece of information she had missed.

"You know as much as I do. Trem and the fairies nonsense." Dant's smirks grew.

"I mean *really*."

Dant paused. His gaze rolled towards the elders and oracles, grouped together in a circle by the bridge. Then his eyes swiftly locked with her own. "Fame is nothing but some slight favor of the most fickle. The elders rule, the celebrities beneath them draw the public in one direction or another. Helpful little magnets collecting pieces of iron into a more concentrated solution. And solutions, Kidra, answers, the likes of us will never have."

Kidra approaches the room that was Dant's and Sulsu's. A jug half filled with a translucent mixture of jet sits unfinished on the small table. A pillow sits on the floor next to a fainting couch. Kidra sits down on the corner of the bed. Rhode remains in the doorway, appearing frightened of both the room and the rest of the tower. Kidra reaches out to Rhode, motioning to her to come into the room.

"You can stay here," Kidra says, getting up. "I'll make sure you stay safe." Kidra puts her arms around Rhode in a terse and stately manner then leaves the room. Her eyes scan the brightly lit dual staircases down to the entrance way. The stained glass window above the doorway is quite rudimentary. The broken image attempts to display the tower and the large bridge that it protects, as well as flames of white light. Kidra lets her eyes focus on the darkness behind the images. The cloudy skies give no hint of the bright stars behind them. And they pay no heed to her yearning to see them. Her thoughts move to Isse, who she has not seen since she was led away by a s'chana keeper. She winces at the memory of the myrlorx in the lower quarters. Her thoughts are interrupted by footsteps coming up the stairs. She sees Bal's head come into view and then his ceremonial robes, worn with contempt.

"Did you gather that you are to replace Dant?" He asks as he alights the last few steps. "It seems things have all worked out in your favor." He grins at her. Kidra restrains a scoff. She remembers Dant's words outside. "Don't tell me you're not happy with this outcome?"

Kidra raises an eyebrow. She knows how Bal could manipulate situations, form them in his heavy hands like clay. "What were you doing at the apartment, Bal?" She is shocked by the words even as she says them.

"What do you mean?"

"The walls were covered in blood. You wouldn't have anything to do with that, would you? You wouldn't have been trying to interfere with an active investigation were you?" She watches as the look of realization takes hold. His participation, or at least some sort of complicity, in whatever had happened in that room is certain. "Look Bal, I won't go asking questions, requesting further investigation, if you leave us alone. I don't need another babysitter."

Bal smiles. "Well, don't you have it all planned out. I don't have a problem going back to Hant or elsewhere. I have enough people on the ground."

"Good."

"I even had one in the woods."

Kidra tilts her head.

"You did have a chance to meet my niece Antrisse, didn't you?"

Kidra stares at him, unable to process his words.

He motions to the entrance way below. "The elders will want to prepare you for tomorrow's statement. And the last ceremony, no doubt."

Kidra watches him disappear down the long upper corridor and into a room across. She feels her shoulders sink. Her defiance she had felt so strongly only hours ago was for naught. She wishes to devise some sort of plan, but her body feels weak and drained. She feels alone with her familiar shame, this time at her relief in the prevale of the status quo.

Part 2

32
Cymt
02/09/2500 2:31PM
31 Days

Kidra approaches the white castle of Cymt. The surface appears as ice, reflecting the equally white surroundings with a magical shear. Each tower, each battlement, reaches upwards in a tapering, indulating fashion, as if made by inverse icicles dripping from their first confrontation with the Sun of an early spring. The rotation of the eurasian tectonic plate after the Time of the Sun had caused this continent of Cymt to sit securely north and Kidra feels the results in her every cell. She shivers again. Although she had been told that the icy temperatures of Cymt were more often than not calm and dry in comparison to the bitter cold of Sularian nights, she has found these first few hours difficult to bear. She tries to wake her numb limbs as today's meeting has a great deal at stake.

The bridge battle with the myrlorx had only served to increase the animosity of the Cymtian elders towards Great Sular. This is the first time since the incident that High Elder Nwirin Nnion had acquiesced to anew the dialogues between the nations. Kidra's popularity has been fading quickly since her oracleship began and she feels herself losing the respect of the elders daily. She feels the weight of this mission and the need, for her benefit, to successfully negotiate the joint eldership.

"Nearly there, Oracle Pi Soulde," the navigator says. Kidra's last name was changed at the request of the elders. Though this was not an uncommon practice among oracles, distancing Kidra from Dant was a priority of the elders after the light ceremony five months ago. As they travel nearer to the castle, the movements of the vehicle become smoother. The icy moat that surrounds the castle requires specialized rhee cyrbs, vehicles designed to glide smoothly above the snow and ice that engulf this land. Kidra sees the large white door, though almost mistakes its edges as delicate snow carvings.

"The door is shut," she says to the navigator. "Are we not expected?"

The navigator laughs, "Cymtians would not survive if we kept our homes exposed." He stops the vehicle and taps the front screen to open Kidra's door. The cold hits her with a sudden blow.

When she catches her breath again, she says, "Yes, I see what you mean. This is much worse than at the bridge."

"The coast isn't as bad, but the castle is much further north, you see," he shouts against the raging wind.

"How will we get in?"

"I'm afraid I must wait here for you, Oracle Pi Soulde. Go towards the door."

Kidra turns again to the vast door. As she walks closer, the delicate design appears more labyrinthine. As she faces the center of the door, a knocker comes into view. She stares at it for a moment before holding her wrists together. Her long gloves make it all the more difficult to grab hold of it but at last, she brings it down to a delicate knock. The door swings outward with a slow heavy movement and Kidra has to run backwards to avoid getting hit. Her lungs fill with the cold air and she feels a hot blush rush to her cheeks. She sees a figure in the doorway. The brightness of the interior of the castle darkens the figure in a shadow, but she can see the silhouette of a motioning to come in. She walks quickly inside and hears the loud vibration of the door close behind her. She breathes in the warm air with an invigorating relief.

Turning to the figure, robed in white, she states, "Oracle Kidra Pi Soulde. I am here to dialogue with the High Elder Nwirin Nnion." She bows her head down and removes a small camera from her pocket. It hovers in the air and rotates around her and the robed man. The man nods and proceeds to walk into another room. Kidra moves to follow him, but the man stops her. She is alone in the large entrance way, the camera still hovering around her.

She sees a fire in the corner of her eye and resists the urge to run to it, to warm her frozen body. She walks slowly with forced composure and puts her wrists near the flames. She closes her eyes as the blood rushes back with delight to her extremities. Suddenly, the feeling intensifies and a deep burning pain takes hold. She pulls her arms away but the burning continues in throbs. She keeps her face still, ensuring not to show this pain to the camera.

"You must be careful not to warm your body too soon." The voice to Kidra's right makes her start. Kidra recognises the Cymt high elder instantly. "This type of cold has a tendency to constrict one's blood vessels. Overheating too quickly can be painful."

Kidra nods gently at the man. High Elder Nwirin Nnion is taller than Kidra had imagined, his grossly inflated body dominating the large room. His long beard nearly reaches the floor; Despite these white features, the man somehow juxtaposes, appearing in disarrange, with the pale background of the Cymt room.

"Shall we get to the dialogues then?" He asks in forced jest. Kidra nods and looks around for chairs. Nwirin clears his throat. The cameras continue to swerve, drifting in and out to obtain a three dimensional image of the two. Nwirin flaps his hand to push one of the small cameras away from his face. The dialogues begin with consideration to Tel Bridge.

Kidra feels that the dialogues are going well, having spent hours now discussing one topic after another. Nwirin's answers to her questions are abrupt, but more often than not in agreement with her. A joint eldership is clearly in sight, though Nwirin is obviously not accustomed to such dialogues. Indeed, although Cymtian elders run Cymt in much the same way as the elders in Great Sular, the idea of celebrities, of garnering favor of the public, is foreign to this land. Kidra gets the impression that she is thought of as some strange weakly being to Nwirin. The conversation at last turns to the myrlorx. The elders had told her that the dialogues would hinge on this; The Cymtian's decisions regarding the myrlorx will color the public's view entirely.

"Actually," Kidra says, "The myrlorx population is growing at a fair rate. We now ensure they remain in South Ghi and do not cross our central borders. In fact--"

Nwirin swiftly hits one of the small cameras, causing it to fall from the air onto the floor with a small thud. Nwirin's face has changed. He has sweat dripping from his forehead. Kidra's body becomes rigid. She notices the remaining cameras dim and lower to the floor. The broadcast had been halted. She is unsure if this was initiated by her elders, if Nwirin had done something, or if the signal was disrupted by the increasingly lowering temperature.

"Mniwch nhi! Dln nhi gulay liad!" He stands. "The dialogues are over!" Nwirin speaks with a heavy tone from the back of his throat, his jaw remaining rigid throughout each word. His movements, too, have become rigid and harsh. He leaves the room with heavy footsteps and disappears into another bright corridor. Although confused, Kidra is relieved to be rid of him and free to return, her mission successful. She pulls her robe tightly around her and walks to the front entrance. The door seems even larger than before but she did not want to wait for anyone to assist her in getting out. She pushes the door, leaning forward with her full body weight. When the door opens a crack, she pushes her face out to look for her navigator. Her eyes struggle to adjust to the now dark landscape. She can't see the rhee cyrb and the fresh snow has covered its tracks to or from the castle. Her nose aches with cold and she pulls herself back inside. She breathes out heavily, attempting to rid herself from the remnants of the painful cold. She leans back against the door and awkwardly removes her scroll from her robe with her wrists. She reviews the map of the area. The castle is situated adjacent to a large mountainous region. The path to the bridge involves multiple turns and would be impossible on foot even in less hostile conditions.

"Well."

Kidra jumps. She looks up from the map to see the man who had opened the door.

"Shall I show you your room?"

"My room?"

"You will not be able to travel in such conditions. Come." The man leads her up a wide winding staircase. The higher they go, the brighter the walls become until they are sparkling flashes of pure light. Kidra has to squint to see the man. He motions to a door at the end of a long hallway. Kidra walks towards it, glancing back at the man who is now descending the staircase. Kidra feels relief when she opens the door to a dark unlit room. A great round window displays the darkness of the night. In the distance, she thinks she can see the tower on the other side of the bridge, but that is quite impossible. Rhode is still in that tower. Before Kidra's journey, Rhode had expressed constantly her desire to go to Hant together. She had begged Kidra not to go to Cymt.

"It's dangerous there," Rhode had warned her.

"I can take care of myself." Kidra had ordered the s'chana keepers of Tel Tower to search for Ghli's body in South Ghi. From it, she had obtained her dagger which remains in her ankle holster.

Kidra finds herself growing tired and climbs into the large bed. The night in Cymt is long and cold. The next morning, she looks out her window to see a calm snow and the beautiful blue mountains to the east.

33
The Machine
02/16/2500 11:27AM
22 Days

Rhode presses the soft clay over the multicolored wires of the machine. Mr. Ish Tin's machine had been very inefficient. Its function relied on the increased power afforded to the generator during the light festival. She simply cannot wait for another power surge to get back to the caves. On her return to Mr. Ish Tin's inn, the machine had been dismantled. Mitya apparently knew nothing of the time travel under questioning by the s'chana keepers. Rhode has been working on building a new machine with the same basic elements as Mr. Ish Tin's. This has been primarily

Kidra's project, her personal research as an oracle. Rhode has enjoyed working day and night in this large room below the main floor of the tower. The elders had been distrustful of Rhode's presence, but Kidra had demanded that she stay. Rhode quickly developed a loyalty to Kidra, and felt secure that Kidra would ensure she would remain safe in Great Sular. She has spent much of the last few months trying to spend as much time in Kidra's presence as possible, which has not been difficult with Kidra's near constant clinging.

Rhode wipes the grease from her forehead and takes stock of the room. Nal is sleeping in the corner of the room, in her usual position. Nal had found her again fairly quickly, though still likes to run across the country each evening. Rhode is certain she is the fastest solceros who ever lived. She looks down at the machine. She can see her reflection in the shining metal. She loves that she is no longer marked by her brown dress. Her linen tunic and trousers are permanently stained with grease and clay. It is all Rhode can do to stop Nal from constantly licking off the oil from her arms on a daily basis, though Rhode knows there is little that can damage a solceros. She stands on her bare and now bruised feet and looks at the machine in its entirety. It has an even green glow, similar to Mr. Ish Tin's, but it is still missing sufficient power. It has enough force and connectivity, but it just needs something to bridge the gap. It is much more compact than Mr. Ish Tin's and Rhode is satisfied that she will be able to transport it to Hant when Kidra returns from Cymt. *Cymt*. Even after all these months, just thinking about it sends shivers down her spine. She kneels again, concentrating on the machine to escape the memories.

"Still working on that?" Sulsu says as she walks into the room. Sulsu has a habit of entering rooms within the tower without knocking.

"Hello, Sulsu." Rhode tries not to lose focus on the machine.

"Don't you think at this point you're just wasting time?"

"No."

"As long as you're sure." Sulsu smiles, swirling the glass of jet in her right hand. Rhode has noticed that Sulsu has been becoming more needy, desperate to belong. In the hectic changes of the expanding eldership, the two young women have found themselves trapped in parallel states of uncertainty. "You like to hide out down here, don't you?" Nal awakes in the corner of the room, stretching out her long front claws.

"I wouldn't say I'm hiding…"

"No? Not frightened to be up there with the rest of society? Not scared to be away from Kidra?"

Rhode sighs. She looks at Sulsu and says, "I need to get back to work. It really is important, you know. You haven't been there." She stops and remembers the comfort of the confined spaces between the memory rooms. Even this room seems too wide, like her body will break apart at any second without the supportive architecture of hard stone around it.

"Well, Kidra will be back to you soon enough. It sounds as if the dialogues with the Elder Nwirin Nnion went well."

As Sulsu speaks the name, Rhode feels a nauseating sensation come over her. Her vision becomes stretched, more than she can bear. She feels dizzy, but as if everything has slowed, as if she is trying to move underwater. She cannot hear that name again.

"You won't have to," Kidra had said to her. "You won't have to go back there."

Before Kidra had claimed her oracleship, she had agreed to travel with Rhode to the town just east of Hant, Ciul, to visit her family. The journey had been silent, but she found Kidra's presence comforting. When they arrived at the cemetery, Rhode struggled to find her parents' names. Finally, she gave up, content enough to assume they were buried somewhere beneath the many unmarked grave sites. She was never told how they had died. She has often pondered what it was that had led to their death. Was their affinity with myrlorx discovered by the greater community? Had they shown signs of becoming myrlorx themselves? When Rhode's family was taken away, she was selected for the Mass Relegation. On that day in the cemetery with Kidra and everyday since, Rhode has wished only to go back to the caves.

34
Njuyut

02/19 5:30AM
19 Days

    The sun has yet to rise. The quiet of the early morning is interrupted by the songs of birds, the wind manipulating the leaves of the many pine trees, and the stirrings of the sleeping children. It is glorious. The heaviness of the night has given rise to the lightness of the day's beginning. He can still see the beautiful orb of the moon. He straightens his body, feeling the release in his muscles, and begins a silent prayer. Soon the rest of the island dwellers will wake and the joint prayer can begin, as it does each day. Hln stands, his back to the great body of water and the hint of light. The striped Sun is kind to the islands of Njuyut. It is as it has always been. The glow in the ocean near the new bridge gives Hln pause. The disparate people, those on the world's edges, invite evil with their perverse desires to manipulate the natural world.

    The elders of Great Sular have been using small ships to bring large quantities of their 'jet' to the islands. The Njuyutis officially reject this and continue to pour the mixtures into the ocean. Unfortunately, a small number of islanders have been tempted by the substance. Despite warnings by the high priestesses, Hln suspects that several bottles were taken before the most recent dumping. He is at a loss of what to do, besides waiting for guidance from the high priestesses. Those who bring the jet have taken up a temporary residence on the island. It vexes him that they must share their resources even for a transitory moment. Still, what can he do? The land is as much theirs as it is his. He sees one now. The woman exiting the tent is short compared to the Njuyutis. Her pale hair is twisted in multiple tight knots. She is quieter, easier to accept. The neighboring tent rustles. The other one exits, his loud waking groans strike Hln as churlish. They are whispering to one another again. The man re-enters his tent while the woman walks towards Hln. That man has rarely left his tent. And all the better for the island.

Hln sits down on a large rock and looks up to her as she approaches him. She smiles. Hln knows that she has grown to appreciate the ways of the Njuyutis.

"Sky above and ground below," she greets him with the traditional reception in her broken Njuyuti.

"Sky," he answers casually.

"It looks like we will have another beautiful day." She points to the waves spilling the rising tide. "Perhaps a storm tonight."

Hln smiles back. "Let's hope so." Storms are common this time of year. Rejecting of the lohqra liquid, the islanders rely on fishing to ensure adequate sustenance. The large waves have often brought them a bounty of fish, though their catches have been significantly diminished since the construction of that abominable structure.

"I understand the meeting of the high priestesses is underway. Do you know what the topic is this time?"

Hln laughs to himself. Such people will always be loyal to Great Sular, as if it is an entity in itself, as if it as a thing exists at all. "You can guess with enough accuracy."

"Mmm." Her smile falters. "I will leave you to your prayer."

"You will not stay for the morning prayer?"

"Although I'd love to," her voice lowers, "I must wait for the boats." She looks down to the sandy beach and she walks towards the dock at the far side of the island. Hln laughs to himself again.

He sees a few rising faces of the islanders and stands to welcome them to a new day. The prayer is a magnificent sequence of synchrony. Reaching towards the moon as it dissolves into daylight, they dance. When the moon is no longer visible, they disperse to their activities. The boats are pulled out to sea and the fishermen become miniature fragments nearing the horizon. Hln remains on the island, hoping to speak with his mother should the meeting conclude today. He looks up to the tall man made hill of stone on which sits the temple. The high priestesses may well remain there for many more days until they reach a decision. He looks around to ensure no one watches him, and then he ascends the great hill. It is by no means forbidden to go near the temple, but it is frowned upon to disturb the high priestesses during periods of reflection. From a young age, Hln has felt exempt from such etiquette and, though he is more discreet as an adult, still behaves in these imprudent ways. The vegetation flourishes high on the hill, seeping through the many cracks in the stone and winding upwards towards the sky. Small berries hang off the end of a long branch. He plucks one and brings it to his mouth. He winces at the sourness of it but perseveres with the bite. When he reaches the entrance of the temple, with its heavy stone doors, he presses his ear to the door, attempting to feel the vibrations that would indicate footsteps, the end of the meeting, but the rock is still. Hln sits down on the ground and takes in the view of the island. He can see a large boat from Great Sular pulling away from the dock with difficulty against the crashing sea. The woman is walking along the edge of the water, looking at the rampant waves. He frowns at the Njuyut people's growing reliance on Great Sular. Even their children are sent here from boats of Ji. At least his people still reject the blood transfusions, the second skins, and the cheap tricks to prolong life. Hln feels the vibration beneath him and excitedly looks back to the door.

"Sky above, Hln," says Irho as she steps gracefully out of the temple.

"How was it, mother?"

Irho purses her lips and kneels down next to Hln, her gaze falling on the woman by the dock. "We have reached an agreement on what must be done."

35
Hologram

02/19/2500 4:30PM

She knew he had every intention of deceiving her. His tall body and sharp features were almost attractive in a pathetic way. He seemed unintelligent. She felt she could afford to play with him. His Cymtian accent is obvious but his Sularian is perfect.

"My dear," he says. He has called her this often.

In time, her guards fell away. In his eyes she thought she could see a certain desperation, a hope that she would truly love him. He was interested in her, always her, never his own culture. He kisses her again, in short, annoying mashings of lips. She pushes him away, her hand on his bony chest.

"Don't do it like that." She releases her hand and lets his body fall back. "Let them linger."

He moves over her and brings his lips to hers again, restraining himself. Sulsu smiles and wraps her arms around him. She pulls him down onto her. He pulls away and stands.

"I need to go."

"Stay for just a little bit more."

"No," he says with a certain vacantness in his expression. She tries to bring her eyes to meet his but she can't. He finds his shoes and puts them on. Sulsu stands and plants herself before her closet. All of her belongings from Ji had been brought to this little room beneath the tower. She pulls out a black and white dress.

"Would this look nice?" She feels a desperation for his attention.

"Fine," he replies. "I will return later." He kisses her on the forehead and leaves through the main door.

Sulsu lets herself fall back onto the bed. She closes her eyes and imagines their life together, her, him, and Dant. Dant wouldn't mind. Dant doesn't care about her like that. And he can so easily adapt to her own life. The door slides open again. Sulsu shoots up, excited for his return, but is disappointed to see Dant, brought by a s'chana keeper. He is to be escorted during all of his brief outings. As is she. She reaches for her jug of jet and pours the slow moving current into her large glass.

"I saw *him* leaving." Dant's eyes are wider than Sulsu has ever seen them.

"Yes, I'm sure you did." Sulsu feels the rush of electricity through her body as the jet enters her bloodstream. "You'll get used to him."

"I certainly hope not."

The elders had dissolved Dant's marriage to Kidra in order to advance Kidra's standing as the new oracle. They had refused to do the same with his marriage to Sulsu. She had considered revealing Dant's role in her father's death but resolved that at this point Dant's status could sink no lower. Instead, she continues to drink more and more jet. It seems to make everything better. Sulsu hears the vibration of the call on the short cylindrical holoconf in the corner of the room.

"Kidra again?" Sulsu asks, placing her veil over her face playfully. Dant ignores her and walks quickly to the buzzing device. He presses his foot onto the side, causing it to wobble slightly. The noise stops and a flash of light radiates upwards. Kidra stands before them, or at least a perfect holographic projection. Kidra is presumably controlling the projection from Cymt, based on her heavy robes and wrapped arms.

"Dant," Kidra smiles.

Sulsu rolls her eyes and pulls her legs up onto the bed.

"Yes, Kidra? Can I help?" Dant asks tersely, though Sulsu knows that Dant cherishes his conversations with Kidra. Their secret meetings have gone on throughout Kidra's oracleship.

"Dant," Kidra says again, glancing behind her. "I'm still in Cymt."

"Are the dialogues not going well? Everything seemed to plan on the broadcast."

"He has accepted. The joint eldership is going ahead."

"You must be relieved."

Kidra nods, her eyes unfocused. "I'm ... I have to stay here for the time being. Neither the elders nor... Nwirin wish to arrange another vehicle as of yet." Dant looks back at Sulsu. Sulsu bites her lower lip. Why would the elders want Kidra out of the way? Kidra must have caught the look between them because she continues, "There is something else... It seems that I am pregnant."

The shock of her words echoes through the rooms. Sulsu feels sharp embarrassment pulsing through her. No one in civilization has been capable of reproducing for hundreds of years. In fact, the new skin should have depleted all of her internal organs by now. Children come from the forest. Even the knowledge of the myrlorx fertility is something that Sulsu pushes from her mind. The revolution of it. Sulsu sinks deeper into the bed, fixing her eyes on the ceiling's cheap textured gray wallpaper.

"And the elders know?" Sulsu hears Dant reply. Kidra must have nodded, given Dant's exasperated sigh. "How could this be? My god! What is that scar?"

"The myrlorx. On my first night with them I woke up with new blood and this."

Dant is silent for some time. "They'll spin it somehow. They always do."

"Dant, I don't want them to spin this. I want to get out of here!" Kidra whispers. " You must be able to do something or..."

Sulsu feels Dant's eyes on her. "She won't be of any help. They've already got to her with the jet and some play thing." Sulsu pushes herself upright on the bed and glares at Dant. She sees Kidra's worried expression. "Oh she won't say anything," he adds. Sulsu knows she couldn't tell anyone if she wanted to, the embarrassment is hard enough to bear as it is.

"I need to get back to Rhode. What am I going to do?"

"There is something going on all right," Dant lowers his voice. "There is more tension between the elders and the oracles here. I thought that the dialogues would resolve that, but I overheard more arguments in the conference room only earlier today. The so-called harmony is no more."

"Are you still in touch with your father?"

"In touch? That's a way to put it. He still sends me letters from the islands, bragging. Apparently Isse is a better heir than I ever could be." Kidra tenses at the mention of Isse. Her gaze drifts off to the side.

"I can see more crates are flying in. They have been sending in more jet. Just to the castle." There is another pause in the conversation. Sulsu considers why the elders would want Kidra to drink more of it. "I should go. Please Dant, do what you can. Or at least…"

"I'll let you know if I hear anything."

Kidra smiles weakly. Her image flickers once and then is pulled back down to the floor. Dant taps the cylinder with his foot and then tips it over. This is said to prevent rogue holograms from developing. Sulsu rolls her eyes at the superstitious motion.

36
Glow
02/20/2500 9:20AM
18 Days

Nal presses her horn against Rhode's arm, prompting Rhode to scratch her furry neck. With her other hand, Rhode taps her rench absentmindedly over the machine, trying to bring her focus back to the calculations. She is closer to making a link between the microchips and the wave stream of the joint memories. Last night, in attempting to dilute the current fuel, she had used the leftovers of Sulsu's glass of jet. The light had sparked a power upsurge that nearly opened the portal, but there is still something missing. Teven was right; Without the ncreased electricity output, it is certainly tricky to access to say the least.

She hears a knock at the door. This is unusual. Most of the time, people come and go as they please. The elders speak of her as if she isn't even there. They walk past her, into her, through her room below the tower. The tower seems to be buzzing with new information, new worries every day. They had mentioned Kidra's pregnancy yesterday as if it was something everyone knew already. It was a shock for Rhode to hear. Her place here is slipping away quickly. She stands and looks to the door.

"Yes?" She asks. The door slides open, revealing Elder Crih Yulah standing before her, his pale blue robes contrasting the dark hallway behind him.

"Rhode, still working away?"

"Of course."

He glides to the room, his scanning gaze landing on Nal with a disapproving scowl.

"Do you have news on Kidra's return?" She asks tentatively.

"We've greater problems than chauffeuring Kidra." Crih smiles and takes a few steps closer to Nal. Nal shifts her head upwards. "We are trying to unite an empire. Increasing myrlorx sightings are being reported by the day. Not in groups but one by one. Meanwhile, our power grid is faltering." He touches the machine and is immediately revolted by the damp condensation over it. "And I'm sure your experiments aren't helping."

"It's not attached to the power grid--"

"Of course," he says sarcastically. "In any case, the elders have agreed that we can no longer support Kidra with this ... project. Once your new papers are in order, you'll be back to Cymt where you belong." He stares hard at Nal and then walks out leisurely, leaving the door open wide.

Nal cowers in the corner next to the machine, touching against it with her horn. Rhode drops to the floor, resting her arms on her knees. As she looks up at the machine, her eyes widen. She finally sees an increase in the glow of the machine. It won't be long now before the portal to the caves can be open permanently.

37

Florid
02/24/2500 9:59AM
14 Days

Kidra turns to the hovering cameras, tilts her head back, and smiles. Her new blue gloves have built-in finger orthotics, positioned in a permanent claw-like grip and useful for little more than holding a glass. She brings the long glass of jet up to her face and eyes the suspended black vapors.

"One more sip, Kidra," Whulè says from behind the bright lights of the cameras.

Kidra brings the glass to her lips, the smile still rigidly in place. She takes a sip. The bitter taste is swallowed in a hard lump. Kidra feels the rush of it rise upwards in her body. She looks directly into one of the cameras and says, "Florid Jet, by Kidra."

"Good. Fine." The oracle says.

Kidra lets her face fall as the cameras power down and the lights dim. She still desperately wants to leave Cymt and her thoughts compulsively circle around potential escape plans. The emptiness of the tower is overwhelming. During the day, she drinks lohqra with Nwirin and his assistant in silence. Often they look at her, as if to speak to her, but they don't. She dare not leave her room when the sun goes down. And without a vehicle she is trapped in this far away cold land until the elders deem it suitable for her to leave.

"When are you going to bring me home?"

"You've been a good oracle, Kidra. Don't push things now. Dant never really understood what we needed from him. Personhoods are useless in this sort of role. You need to disappear. You are an oracle now. That alone is your identity."

Kidra did not know she had any identity of her own, but the sudden confrontation of it being taken from her right here in this desolate castle is more than she can bear. *I don't want to be a thing, an instrument with morals barely held together with a handful of transglutaminase.* She looks towards Whulè, trying to look him in the eyes, but before she can say anything, he turns and walks away, his hologram disappearing into nothing. She sighs and clicks off the holoconf. Kidra feels the boldness in her atrophy. She is glad that Whulè left her with her anger unspoken. Despite everything, she still wants her oracleship. She knows the oracles are being overtaken by the elders and that cooperating is her only hope of remaining in their favor. She finishes the jet in a single swallow. Footsteps from the outside hallway cause her to pause. Nwirin's assistant must be lurking about again. She sinks to the floor and pours another glass of jet.

"You look paranoid." Kidra jumps. Dant's image is in the room. She must have accepted his hologram when she turned off Whulè's. "More jet?"

"It's warming. Cymt is all but unbearable."

"Have the elders been? I heard you were advertising your own personal brand of poison."

"Just Whulè."

"Have you gotten used to the Cymt religion yet? It will be blended in with Great Sular soon enough once the coalesce goes forward. I heard it's all ancient forms of personal prayer in Cymt. That should make the light ceremonies a bit more streamlined."

"It's not much of a religion. No ceremonies, religious attire is supposed to be toned down out of respect for the Cymtian elders, but the high elder certainly doesn't meet with the public." She pauses and looks to the floor. "Have you found out anything yet?"

Dant sighs. "The elders and the rest of the oracles ... they are just planning, talking, planning, like they always do."

"Dant, what am I going to do? I thought I would have more ... power as an oracle."

"Don't be silly, Kidra. They used us for our status. The utility of our status hides our personhood to them. They look at us and see a mirror. Their most hated parts of themselves are reflected onto our faces by their own imagination, so they can be cruel to us. We are nothing to them. I don't know what you are going to do, but whatever it is, I suggest you do it soon. I wouldn't be surprised if the elders will be rethinking your eldership soon."

"They know I value this eldership. The machine will be advantageous in time."

"I would forget that little project if I were you. The elders haven't been so tolerant of it lately."

"But what about Rhode?"

"All you talk about lately is Rhode. Don't you care about anything else? Hasn't anyone else in your life registered?

Don't you think about Ghli? Don't you think about your son?"

"I can't talk to you about anything." Without getting up, Kidra reaches for the holoconf alternator and disconnects Dant's hologram. She leans back against the bed and rests her hands on her enlarged abdomen. She wishes she could meet that mad Njuyuti woman again, go to the islands and confront her. She blames the woman for her current predicament. This unnatural gravid state must be more than simple misfortune. She thinks back to the early days of humanity when humans would routinely bear children naturally. Such a state was thankfully interrupted for all but the myrlorx. *Yes, the myrlorx. I need to understand.*

Kidra rises and looks out the great window. The blue and white of the Cymtian landscape sparkle. She has to squint to make out the crates flying towards her in the distance. *I need to see it in the caves myself.*

38
A Return to the Caves
02/24/2500 2:44PM

Rhode gasps with relief as she sees the familiar green glow encase the room. Nal gently shakes her head and the glow flickers. Rhode has attached Nal's horn to a tube connecting to the machine. The addition of jet in combination with the power of a solceros horn is enough to open the portal, at least temporarily. Rhode kisses Nal on the cheek and presses her cheek against Nal's. Although Nal does not seem to be in pain, Rhode feels a surge of guilt over using her like this.

"I won't be gone long this time, Nal. You'll need to stay out so I can come back. Hopefully with more information on how to keep the portal open for good." Rhode takes a deep breath in and climbs up the ladder she has situated over the portal. "Wish me luck." She jumps.

The flash of green is brilliant around her and consumes her vision. While awaiting the familiarity of the stone walls, she finds herself immediately in another memory. She is sitting on the damp street, under a flickering street light. To her left is the machine. She looks up to see the street light above her is broken. She looks at her hands and realizes the flickering glow is coming from her own skin. She is breathing quicker now. In a rush, she turns to the machine, the pedals of which are turning madly, unmanned. A man is looking down at her from the window above. *Teven*. Before Rhode knows what to do, he is falling towards her. She braces herself and the machine's glow grows into a flash of light that obstructs her vision completely. In an instant she is out of the memory, with a harsh jolt that she had forgotten. She is again within the tight confines of a narrow crevice, her shoulders compressed against the walls. The darkness around her is stale. It is somehow not as she remembered at all. She puts her hand to the cold, wet limestone and lets it guide her forward. The slippery mud beneath her pulls her back on herself with every movement of her legs, but she continues inch by inch.

She looks around her, willing her eyes to find *something* in front of them, some hint of a turn or a fleeting memory. She doesn't know how far she has managed to pull herself forward or how long she has been trying. At last, she can see a glimmer in front of her. It could be a memory or the shine of a room. She lowers her head to squeeze forward, hoping that the glimmer will still be there when she looks up again. The tunnel's walls give and she can relax her shoulders. She looks up as she pulls the rest of her body from the cramped space and smiles at the steady stream of light. She can see now that it is coming from a room above. She feels around for something she can use to pull herself upwards. Her hands slip against the rock walls above her. She pushes her head upwards to get a better look and is taken aback at the expanding stream of light. Her surroundings illuminate and then fade into another memory.

Rhode feels the rough jostling of the train before she recognises the setting. A sense of dread pours through her from deep inside. The train's sudden stop causes the surrounding passengers to rise and walk forward to the exit. She feels herself rising and exiting the train behind them. Already, the others are far ahead of her, their footprints prominent in the snow. She reaches for her shoe which is folded at the back. Holding the shoe, she feels herself straightening it and redonning it. A tall man in white robes, who is one of the leaders of the group, stays behind, seemingly urging her playfully to catch up with the rest of the group. The man asks about her shoes.

"I got them from the Ves neighborhood, of all places," Rhode hears her reply.

She follows the group who are moving faster still along a public pathway in the small frozen town. The man in the white robe smiles at her and says something in Cymtian. She and the man lose sight of the main group. He motions for her to follow him into a shop. As they enter, walking side by side, the shop owner makes a comment in Cymtian and gives her a bemused look. The group leader holds up a small bag of sweetened chetay berries from a shelf and looks at her questioningly. She nods. She turns her attention to a stack of plain dresses. She pulls a dress tightly around her then laughs. Suddenly, the man becomes angry, hitting his fist against the table. Rhode feels the familiar confusion, along with the nonsensical urge to soothe the situation, waving over her, like a moment of deja vu. Rhode feels herself moving closer to him, as if to ask what's wrong. He is getting more worked up and walks to the back of the shop. Rhode feels the following footsteps below her with the increasing need to assuage. In the back of the shop, she sees an open door. Rhode wants to stop this, she must, but she feels the body she is trapped within becoming deeply afraid. She tries to move the body, get away, like she could in the memory of Elder Ish Tin. But, as the fear pulses through her, she feels herself becoming placid, passively paralyzed to someone else's will. She closes her eyes as he holds her shoulders and pulls her into the small room. As he presses himself over her, the memory fades and Rhode is jolted back into the cave.

Rhode is upright, still staring upwards to the bright room, momentarily unable to move. Even the worry over being trapped again within her memory isn't enough for her to move any faster than slow singular motions. Breathing rapidly, she crawls backwards, away from the room. Despite being out of the memory, the images still haunt her as she crawls forward within the dark tunnel. It hadn't been a time she had wanted to remember and to see it again in such detail is more than she can bear. She attempts to move forward but the tunnel walls have become narrower still. As her lungs fill with air, her back and chest press against the stone. She is wedged in completely. She feels her heart beating faster. Panic sets in. Everywhere, she is trapped.

She, and the rest of the children of the Mass Relegation, had boarded the train at Orsaf following their journey by ship to Cymt. She had felt so alone during the journey. Maybe they all did on that boat. The sense of importance she had felt for that brief period of time might be what is most sickening. *What if they send me back? Back to that awful routine, like an unthinking zombie.* It wasn't the ordinary life for an immigrant to Cymt, but it became her normal. The waiting became her life, waiting in nervous anticipation because with each second that went by the anticipation of the torment only grew. He waited for her outside her camp every day and she felt that she could not refuse. There wasn't even a question in her mind. Every day, the others would look at her, judge her, alienate her further. They simply thought her pious, that she was training to be an oracle in the hopes to go back to Great Sular eventually. When the opportunity to go to Great Sular arose, due to her age and the new visitation policy, she left for the boat without telling him. She has tried desperately not to remember Elder Nwirin Nnion and the paralyzing nature of his presence. The authority of his control is far more daunting than the monstrous attributes of the myrlorx.

She feels her breathing slow. She shifts her body and is relieved to feel herself moving forward. Soon, the tunnel widens again.

39
Escape
02/24/2500 5:06PM

Sulsu feels the cool wind against her face. She uses her left hand to keep her long hair by her side, fighting against the strong currents of air. She rests her right hand on his warm arms, which are wrapped around her middle. Dant, escorted by a s'chana keeper, approaches from the back entrance of the tower.

"Flaunting your weak-kneed disposition in public again?" Dant mutters loudly.

"It's hardly public, there are no towns for miles." Sulsu laughs.

"Yes. You learned that the hard way, didn't you?"

Sulsu frowns. She lets her gaze fall to the vast emptiness of land visible to the west. She thinks about what it would be like to try to leave again. She feels the arms around her tighten, as if he knew what she is thinking. She had tried to escape the tower soon after Dant's arrest. She had stolen a vehicle from the elders and driven off onto a main road, some hours away, in the middle of a green and mountainous landscape. She was well on her way to Hant when the vehicle slowed. The road became steeper beyond what she had imagined. When the car finally stopped, it came as no surprise. She resolved to travel the rest of the way on foot. As she climbed upwards on the steep road, the hot sun beating down on her, she saw a couple of people, a man and a woman, entering the road from a hole in the fence. She looked beyond them and saw a trail over a steeper hill. The couple laughed and walked towards her. It seemed that they had been hiking, traveling for the fun of it. The man seemed familiar and she was asked to continue her journey with them. They continued on the journey together up the steep road. In time, they came to a house belonging to the woman's aunt. Sulsu was invited inside for lohqra liquid. After being inside for some time, a sense of fear took over. Moving through room to room, she heard the woman and her aunt speaking about her. They had recognised her as Dant's wife and were planning on having her arrested. She resolved to leave on her own before anyone could notice. As she gathered up her belongings and walked to the front door, the man walked up to her. She asks him if he would escort her out, so she would know the women could not accuse her of taking anything. He agreed, seemingly amiable to her. They walked to the door together and she felt a camaraderie with him. She asked if he would like to come with her, to get away from these gossiping women. He seemed to have considered it for a minute before declining and letting her continue on her way. After walking for some time, Sulsu realized he was following her. He offered to drive her to Hant in another vehicle and she accepted. In the vehicle, she remembered where she had recognised him from: a s'chana keeper from the tower, though off duty. He took her directly back to the tower. As they sat in the vehicle in front of the tower, Sulsu had felt her petulance push back at the situation. She started insulting him and threatening to leave again. The man had interrupted her with a kiss. It was more of a distraction than any sort of passion but was apparently enough to pacify her. Now she goes where she likes, escorted by her own personal s'chana keeper. But, there is nowhere she wants to go to but upwards.

"We should really think, Dant, about having another allotting ceremony. I'm sure a child would help our social standing "

"You must be completely deluded. There's no going back from this." Dant snaps his fingers at the s'chana keeper next to him, prompting him to follow Dant as he starts walking meagerly around the tower, his daily constitution.

"You can't let her stay in charge. She'll have all the myrlorx killed for revenge for her son."

Dant stops and looks at Sulsu. "If Kidra did that, I'm sure she would only become more popular."

"More popular perhaps but with a declining population in Great Sular, what would that amount to?"

"You give her far too much credit, Sulsu. The elders will out the oracles soon enough anyway."

"Don't you care? Don't you want the opportunity to do something? I do. People's humanity could be destroyed. Don't you care?"

"Care?" Dant scoffs. "Never in my life did anyone care for me. I could live or die. My brother with his false charms, he left. Even my adoring public were so quick to turn away."

"Cagh died at sea during the pre-releg war. And your public were probably pretty miffed with all the attempted murders. You have some selective memory. Take *some* responsibility."

"All memory is selective. That's the difference between people, individuals."

"Oh, go for your walk, Dant." Sulsu walks towards the bridge, her s'chana keeper still holding her by the waist. She stops as she sees the beauty of the water. Leaning back, she takes in the darkness of the water on the faraway horizon. Her eyes move across the surface to that under the bridge.

The water under the bridge seems shallow, as if it is drying before her eyes.

40

Seven Crossing
02/25/2500 4:17PM
13 Days

Kidra crawls forward, keeping her head lowered. The footsteps behind her have stopped. She is nearly there, to the lower level of the tower. Her escape from the Cymt castle had been opportunistic. She had awoken in her room much earlier than usual. It had been unusually cold overnight and she had woken multiple times throughout. Upon seeing another shipment of jet coming towards her from her window, she seized her chance. She had managed to sneak down the grand staircase without being seen or heard. The brightly lit castle was eerier than usual. She had paused at the large door, concerned that any movement would wake Nwirin and that that would be the end of her plan. Gathering her strength she pushed the door forward, her body building up to a slow run. She held her breath through the freezing wind and hurled herself into the dark moonlight. The shipment of jet was being emptied into the cellar through the entrance by the automated drone. As it lowered to the ground before closing the empty container, Kidra rushed towards it. She maneuvered her way into the empty shell just as it was ascending. She struggled to stay balanced as the drone flew quickly through the cold air. The little protection that the crate provided against the cold was hardly enough to protect her skin from the wind.

The speed continued to increase. Kidra pulled her feet towards her core, protective of her remaining digits. She moved her feet and arms up and down and kept her cloak closely around herself for the long journey. Now, her body aches. She is still frightened to look at her still numb feet.

Focussing on the task at hand, Kidra listens against the small back door of the tower's lower quarters. She discerns no sound waiting on the other side. She finds the door itself is open. She feels an immediate disappointment as she steps back inside the tower. This is not her home. The elders are as much of a danger to her as Nwirin. She must find another escape. But, first: Rhode. The passageway seems darker than she had remembered it. *Which room was Rhode's lab?* She stops suddenly at the sound of footsteps approaching. Rushing into the nearest open door she can see, she finds herself face to face with a myrlorx.

Kidra backs away, pressing her back against the wall of the small room. The myrlorx looks at her weakly and then lets its gaze fall. Restraints are fastened around its hands and feet, both of which seem to droop with the weight. Kidra looks at the wretched creature. Whatever sort of experiment the elders have orchestrated on it, it has left the thing broken. She notices the multiple patches of blood and feels glad. Ghli had never been safe with them. Despite her better judgment, the years of propaganda, of constant automate messages establishing the myrlorx as inhuman, are still hard to shake. She stays against the wall as the footsteps grow louder. Voices, familiar ones, become audible. They are discussing the growing number of myrlorx. It must be the elders. They speak of the myrlorx as if they matter. *But they do,* she reminds herself. *They are the only thing keeping humanity going.* Even now, here, her mind plays tricks on her. She remembers holding her arms around Rhode's shoulders as they had approached the cemetery all those months ago. She had been trying to explain to Rhode what the myrlorx really are, only to discover her own knowledge is in dire wanting.

"You mean ... they're like humans?" Rhode had asked.

"*Are* humans. As you are," Kidra replied. "Indeed, the same." Rhode looked down to the ground, her cheeks flushed.

"I mean as anyone. No more, no less," she said, trying to soothe the confused look in Rhode's face. "Why it happened, I don't know ... They are fertile, we are not. There is speculation that childbearing will trigger a myrlorx transformation, but I suspect that it is just that, speculation," she offered, though she knew the words were no real answer.

She looks at the myrlorx now. Indeed, it is difficult to want to classify it as human; To admit she was in the same shell that could be deformed into such a shape required more cognitive dissonance than she wished to entertain.

"The skin ceremonies are continuing too," a voice echoes from the passageway.

"Good god." The rough reply is low in tone. "They're doing it to themselves are they?"

"I think it's a good thing. Easier to discern the healthy ones to take."

"Certainly. The timing is perfect. Can't complain about that. Still, quite beastly, really."

Kidra feels a nausea sweeping across her at the idea of the myrlorx cutting into their own flesh, applying the new skins with their primitive surgeries. *And only to separate themselves, to know who is sickly ill with the propensity of their bodies to become inflamed?*

"I suppose it always was. My real concern is you know who."

Kidra hears a laugh. This voice has something of an accent, like some tenant of a regional baile.

"A witness saw the new wife some months back out of the tower ... well it's settled now anyway. My worry is we are not adequately policing our own. Or at least that is what the Cymt leader will say."

"Well, if he wants to police Dant, he's welcome to, surely."

That regional laugh is detectable again. This time it is more of a giggle. The voices are becoming quieter again. Kidra suspects they've passed this little room, with her unnoticed.

"Shall we inspect the bridge? I'm doubtful a dam could do all that."

"See for yourself, Crih."

Kidra hears a door open and then close. They must have left the corridor. The bulge inside of her shifts again, but she cannot afford to waste time. She lets her shoulders relax and leaves the room, relieved to look away from the myrlorx. She tip toes along the corridor, counting each door that she passes. Finally, she comes to the familiar room of Rhode's laboratory. The door is closed. Kidra opens it, expecting to see Rhode fiddling with the misshapen pieces of metal and wires that made up the early model of the machine. Instead, she sees Nal scratching her horn against the glowing machine. In the center of the green energy, above the machine, is a rippling of light, seemingly thick and yet translucent. *She's done it!*

Kidra considers this for a moment. She knows that the answers to her questions, the answers to everything, lie within the grand joint memories of the caves. She has to get inside. Nal looks at her. Kidra backs away, giving the solceros more space. Nal had never shown any affection for her, though their mutual respect manifested in the simple act of leaving one another alone. Kidra looks up. She sees the ladder situated just above the portal's interstice. Rhode had explained to Kidra the need for momentum in order to travel. Without a second thought, Kidra climbs the ladder and lets her body fall into the portal. The resulting blaze of light is stupefying.

For a moment, Kidra thinks the flash has left her blinded, but she soon understands that she now sits within the dark confines of the caves. The stark quiet of the cave is unnerving. She pulls her gloves down and lets her forearms feel the jagged texture of the stone walls. She is in a tunnel, with one way to go. She struggles to crawl forward, unable to balance on her elbows in the tight space. Eventually finding propulsion with her legs, she pushes forward. The regret of her actions washes over her with each painful scrape against the stone. How could she think there are any sort of answers in such a place? The claustrophobia of the tight walls causes her to breath in wide uneven gasps.

In time, just as Kidra has nearly depleted her energy, she comes across a faint light from the floor about one to two meters in front of her. As she crawls closer, she sees that it is a pool of water with a glass-like reflective surface that obscures its depth. *Is this a memory?* She squints and leans forward to better see the glow from behind her own image. Suddenly, the glow increases. The abrupt vacillation from near darkness to shimmering brightness causes Kidra to shut her eyes tight. In her forward position, she feels her proprioception fail her and she falls forward with a splash into the water. She opens her eyes to glittering bubbles spilling out from her mouth. She sinks lower into the water, leaving the surface glow behind and entering a new darkness. Despite her efforts, her lungs gasp for breath. To her shock, she feels herself breathing with ease. She looks upwards at the beautiful allurement of the water's surface.

As she floats further down into the infinite darkness, she feels a rapid growing in her abdomen.

41
Bal
02/25/2500 7:40PM

Isse wades forward towards the approaching boat, up to her waist in the fierce waves of the cold water. She reaches for the cargo carrier as it floats away from the larger ship. She grabs hold of it and forces it around her, such that she is able to push it to land. The shipments of jet have been ample for the island, far too much to be used by the residents even if they were inclined to drink it. Despite her objections, the elders seem to think it couldn't possibly go to waste. Her feet sink into the wet sand as she pushes against the carrier, now scraping against the sand itself. She always hates this part. The sheer weight of it is aggravating. Once the carrier is on dry land, she can remove the boxes of jet piece by piece.

Looking around at the island, Isse feels a twinge. She is always trapped within other cultures for the sake of furthering the elders' majority. Her life has been a cycle of darting around place after place, while her cousin reaped the rewards. Though, not anymore.

"Ouch!" She exclaims as she cuts herself on the corner of the carrier. *These are just getting cheaper and cheaper in their materials.* She sighs and raises her hand above her head, slowly easing her way to her tent with a box of jet in her other hand. The wind is colder today than usual and her wet legs are slow to move with the sting of it. She lets the box of jet fall to the ground outside her tent and pushes her way into her small area of privacy. She picks up her small lighter and brings it to her bloody finger. Cauterizing the wound, she tries not to flinch. The small scars of previous burns around her body will heal in time, but at the moment she feels marked with her labor. The fire islands, as she called them, are home to a multitude of strains of bacteria and viruses unknown to the people of Great Sular. In the beautiful wild of it, the untamed growth that is only guided by the residents, immunity comes from living on the island for the duration of one's life. Travelers here who do not take precautions are likely to die from one of many agonizing ailments. She shakes her hand, trying to distract herself from the throbbing. Against the light of the tent, she sees a shadow approaching.

"Come in," she says with forced cheer. Her attempts to warm the islanders have not gone unnoticed and she intends to persevere, regardless of her mood.

A tall figure pokes his head into the tent. "Good evening, Hln." She forces a smile. Hln's mischievous ways tend to get on her nerves, but Isse does trust him and he has been kind to her throughout her stay. She has considered bringing Hln back to Great Sular for safety once the elder's plan is initiated. "What's wrong?" She asks as she notices that his facial expression is that of sadness. Or is it fear? Guilt perhaps?

"It is Bal." He motions for her to follow him. At first Isse thinks he has committed some transgression. It is true that he has not behaved altogether tactfully during their stay. However when she sees the way Hln is walking, with a dipped forward leaning posture, she reconsiders. This is a somber event. *What has happened to him?*

Bal's tent is as it was when Isse had left him this afternoon. Certainly, there are no obvious signs of foul play. As she enters the tent, the stench is overpowering. The sight of Bal causes Isse to blanch. *This will take time to sort out before getting home to Great Sular.* His rotting face has already blackened and his body is flattened, insects gathering over the necrosed tissue.

42
Blood
02/26/2500 3:59AM
12 Days

Kidra breathes rapidly within the darkness of the water. The pain is only getting worse. Her child will be born here, in the middle of time itself. Kidra feels, in the remnants of her pituitary gland, the triggering of the positive feedback release of oxytocin. The pressure against her cervix increases. With her arm, she feels the scar of the myrlorx incision. She had thought that their reasons were random, like all of their actions, moving on with their lives as they did with vague ideas of what they should or shouldn't have. Now, she thinks differently. It was to *her*. This wasn't a means to let their child live; This was to teach her a lesson. Or a lesson to bring to society. She contracts her body as the pain's rhythm increases to a pulsing. Those wretched creatures never knew her lack of autonomy in this life. She starts swimming upwards, pulling against the heavy water, but she can no longer see the surface. In the depths, she is grabbed by a sense of vertigo; The ideas of up and down become meaningless in the dark waters. She comes into contact with a hard wall. The rocks are sharp against her shoulders. As the pressure inside her increases further, her body spasms forwards, cutting her skin against a protruding rock. The pressure is solid. In desperation, she uses the jagged rock to cut through her second skin to allow the birth. Suddenly, a pocket of light unfolds in front of her. She can see the blood surrounding her. She can see it clearly; The baby is alive and floating in the water. Next to it is the free floating uterus, twisted within the red liquid. The surrounding rocks are glowing against the shimmering blood. Kidra feels weak and closes her eyes.

    She awakens on the cave floor, feeling the relieving pull of gravity once again. She can see the cave walls better now. The dim glow is enhanced by the sparkling stalagmites. She lets her head drop to her right. *Rhode!* There she is, standing before her between two streams of light. Rhode smiles at

Kidra and looks down at the bundle in her arms. It is not until Kidra hears it cry that she realizes what it is. Kidra presses her elbows onto the floor, trying to push herself upright. Her entire body aches, as if gravity is trying to pull her back to the center of the earth. She stands with a struggle and looks down at the blood pooling underneath her.

"We should go now," Rhode says, looking down at the child. "It can't be good for her to be in the caves. Time works differently here. You wouldn't believe how small Nal was when she first ran through the portal."

"How?" Kidra croaks, her throat battling to acclimate the dry air.

Rhode looks around the cave and says, "Follow me." Kidra does, her body shaking violently with every step. Rhode ducks her head under a large stalagmite and disappears into a dark tunnel. Kidra can hear her own breathing hasten. She is reluctant to advance into another area of sinister obscurity, but follows. In the darkness, she feels Rhode's grip on her shoulder. They move quickly and soon come to an area where the cave walls are visible. Many streams of light pour through the cave, radiating many colors. Rhode motions to the precipice in front of them. Below is another endless abyss. Rhode jumps first, still holding the child in her arms. Kidra hesitates before jumping after them, too feeble to formulate another option. The falling feels like nothing at all.

The stun of landing on the floor hits Kidra with an intensity that leaves her speechless. The confusion in her mind is nearly as stupefying. She tries to bring her hand to her head before realizing it is just a stitched over stump. When she tries to stand, she feels the warm blood run from between her legs.

"Do we have a new allotting ceremony to plan?"

Kidra looks up to see three gentlemen in elders' robes staring at her. She turns around and sees a young girl ... *Rhode* ... standing next to a young toddler. "Síofra. Her name." Kidra states automatically. She doesn't understand why, but somehow it is doubtless that that is the child's name. The child smiles at Kidra.

"I think you should have a rest now. Don't you?" The front elder asks in such a way that implies he has no intention of waiting for an answer. He walks up to Rhode and grabs her arm, hard. Another elder moves to a glowing machine and forces a harness around the head of a large solceros.

"Kidra!" Rhode screams, her eyes imploring Kidra to do something. The child looks around, though appears unphased by the fracas.

Kidra looks up to see the first elders standing over her. Everything next happens quickly. Kidra is rushed from room to room, her body having to be dragged by elders and s'chana keepers due to her weakened state. She receives a rapid blood transfusion while drifting in and out of consciousness for days at a time. At times, she sees young

Síofra watching her from behind one corner or another. In her brief moments of clarity Kidra asks what happened to Rhode, to Nal. Her questions are largely unanswered by the guarding s'chana keepers. Finally, an elder approaches her as she lies in bed.

"We need you to make some statements, Kidra. For the sake of the people of Great Sular. This merging has resulted in something of a stir, but I'm sure we can sort that out. What do you say?"

"Where is Rhode?"

"I'm afraid this is a busy business. Cameras first, Rhode second."

Kidra is pulled out of her bed by the s'chana keepers. The blood transfusion has given her more stability on her feet but she is nearly paralyzed with fear of what the elders have planned. Her makeup and hair are done in a rush and result in a face that she barely recognises in the mirror before her. The first public statement involves requesting that the public increase their use of jet in order to offset the previous generator problems. Despite the elders silence on the subject, she gathers that the nonosenic acid is capable of accelerating usable energy. But why the elders would need this, she can't guess.

Day after day, a s'chana keeper escorts her to a set of hovering cameras to read off a large scroll of what to say. After one week, she is finally permitted to leave her room. She walks down the stairway of the tower, the s'chana keepers eying her subtly. On the main floor, she finds Síofra wandering about. Síofra smiles at Kidra with that same smile as before. Kidra rushes to her and picks her up. Síofra is remarkably heavy for her age and looks at Kidra with an uncanny wisdom. Kidra carries her down to the lower level to the corridor of rooms. She pokes her head into door after door, hoping to find Rhode, but they are all empty but for Dant and Sulsu's room, which Kidra avoids. She sighs and walks into Rhode's laboratory, the machine still displaying a dim glow.

Despite her every struggle within them, Kidra feels a pull to return that begins to consume her. She grips into Síofra tighter and the child makes a gentle screech. She looks at Síofra, into her big dark eyes, and touches her forehead to hers. Síofra reaches down to something on a nearby table. Kidra looks closer. It is a glass of jet, only half finished. She looks at the swirling black and then back to the machine.

43
Inniu
03/10/2500 1:02PM
0 Days

Isse clutches the side of the small wooden boat. The archaic motor attached to the underside of it roars through the muting water. The Njuyutis' aptitude for carpentry is impressive, but Isse wishes her boat was larger. The waves seem worse today. Perhaps it is because of her situation, alone in the small boat, with Great Sular still in the distance. The boats in front of her, guided by Njuyutis, are full of basic weapons. The Njuyutis have been building a dam, piece by piece in the dark of the night. Tonight they will enact their plan. Splashes of ice cold water spill into the small boat here and there. The ocean is dark, reflecting the threatening clouds in the sky. There is a voice in her head making vague speculations about being killed at sea, suggesting some secret plot conducted by the Njuyuti priestesses. This, however, is unlikely. She comforts herself with the knowledge that the majority of the Njuyutis are at sea with her, albeit in larger boats. She sees Hln to her right, his boat slowing in order for him to make eye contact with her. He motions with his hands as if to ask if all is still well. She nods. She knows Hln is relying on her. When he gives the signal as they approach Great Sular, she must take action. She had been relieved to, at last, convince at least Hln of her trustworthiness. Her response to Bal's death went a long way there. She feels for Bal's scroll under her cloak, finding its firm presence in her lower pocket.

The hours go by quickly as Isse's mind races through the possible outcomes of her actions. She watches as the mass of Great Sular grows bigger. The lush greenery fills her with nostalgia. She longs to be home again. Such feelings never last, she reminds herself. Her body tenses as she feels the collective anticipation. The Njuyutis before her begin distributing weapons. Their stoic expressions strike Isse as unnatural, as she has only ever seen affable smiles on the islanders' faces previously. The clouds above her part and a ray of sunshine pours over the boats. The large mass of the bridge has been easy enough to ignore for the majority of the journey, but now its shadow is cast over the water to her left, like some underwater beast beginning to surface. A chill falls over her as they approach the tall tower at the bridge's entrance. There are no s'chana keepers in sight. The boats are likely to dock unperturbed. Isse looks for Hln, but can no longer see him in the crowd of boats. The boats knock together and Isse's feet are doused in the salty water splashing over her. She is torn between her desire to get out of these conditions and her reluctance to part from the safe antecedence of the journey.

The boats far in front come to an abrupt stop. She straightens her torso to see the beginning of the dam. There is a resistant drag against her boat as the water beneath becomes shallow. She feels herself eagerly leaning forward, watching the first group of Njuyutis disembark. The engine of her boat rurrs, though Isse's boat does not move forward. She can feel it wedged between several piled logs. She climbs forward and steps over multiple abandoned boats until she is on top of the dam with the islanders.

"Now Isse," Hln shouts to her from deep within the crowd. "Quickly."

Isse retrieves the scroll and backs away from the crowd. She pulls it close, rolling it open with care, and quickly puts the operation into action. She looks up, finding Hln's face in the crowd. As he begins walking hastily towards her, she is certain that her face has given her away.

She hears the sound of the explosion before seeing the crashes of water around her, illuminated with the terrifyingly bright flash. She is submerged. The dam is broken. Isse fights against the waves until she realizes that the current is forcing her to land. She feels the wave hit her against the cliff of Great Sular. Holding tightly to protruding tree roots, her injured body numb with adrenaline, she clamors up to safety. Looking down from the sharp cliff, she sees that the islanders had not been so lucky.

Behind her, s'chana keepers are rushing around like headless chickens, leaving a group of children cowering in fear. She grasps hold of the cliff's edge, wanting to reach out and rectify this tragedy. A sound of heavy breathing causes her to look down. Nearby, to her right, is Hln, hanging on desperately to a salient rock with his legs dangling. Isse gasps. Her body is still. Hln looks at her, his eyes widened. *I cannot!* Suddenly, a girl rushes towards the edge of the cliff. She reaches her hand out to Hln, as if she has enough strength in her to save him. Hln grasps it and grunts as he attempts to press his feet into the rocky cliff.

Hln looks up at Isse. She feels the hurt in his stare. He knows that this is all due to her deception. She had no intention of turning off the power. Nor could she. Even Bal didn't have such power. Instead, she had sent an awaited notification to the Elders warning of the attack. Loyalty means nothing if it is not consistent and yet, Isse feels the shame of her actions sink into her. Hln abruptly forces the girl's hand against the cliff wall. The girl slips forward and lets out a sharp yell. The girl's hand starts to wobble. Hln's hand releases its grip and before Isse can comprehend what is happening, Hln falls rapidly into the crushing waves below. Isse turns to look at the girl. She must be no more than fifteen. The girl brings her hand to her eyes and wipes away her tears, leaving behind smudges of blood with her injured hand.

44
In Hiding
03/14/2500 11:01PM

Sulsu looks at the wall. Its gray paint is already beginning to peel. She grips onto a hanging strand and pulls it free, looking back at it with disgust. The disdain she has for this tiny room is even greater than her hatred for her first room on the higher level. This overpowering smell of overused bleach to cover up the musty smell of pre-used building materials combines poorly with the artificial floral fragrance that Dant had requested in a vain attempt to pacify Sulsu's protests. All of the smells swirl together like some behemoth monstrosity floating invisible in the air. She walks back to the bed, picking up her glass of jet on the way. She brings the glass to her lips, knowing that the slur it is causing is revealing her accent all the more. She looks defiantly at Rhode who is watching as she takes another sip. Although Rhode has got on her nerves, Sulsu enjoys the feeling of superiority brought by hiding her here. It hasn't been particularly difficult to keep her from the elders, now that she has convinced her s'chana keeper guard that he is in love with her. Getting Rhode out of that predicament had been the tricky part.

    Rhode had been grouped with the New Mass Relegation children to be taken to Cymt. It had been a large group in the very small quarters of a newly built building close to the bridge's entrance. The look of the building absolutely paraded its shoddy workmanship, but Sulsu supposed the elders did not wish to waste any time. Poor pathetic Rhode had been stuck in that small room, cramped against other poor hapless souls. It was lucky for the elders that they were alerted to the virus outbreak by the underground sensors. The alarm had awoken Sulsu in the middle of the night. She snuck out of bed and followed the sounds. The elders were there, rushing around, trying to turn off the alarm. The whole thing had piqued her curiosity enough for her to follow them as they set the building on fire. They ignored her, as they often do, even without her s'chana keeper, and went back into the tower for safety. As the walls of the burning building collapsed, she saw Rhode stumbling forward, coughing violently. It had been difficult to get Rhode to the back entrance of the tower without being seen, but not impossible. The commotion of the fire dominated the dark of the night. When she had walked into a s'chana keeper, she was relieved to see it was her s'chana keeper. Together, they hid Rhode away. The elders must assume she had died in that fire with the rest of the sickly children.

A knock at the door causes Rhode to jump. Sulsu rolls her eyes. Her s'chana keeper now knocks before anyone enters the room, giving Rhode time to hide under the bed. Sulsu lifts up the dust ruffle for Rhode to slide under, which Rhode does swiftly. Dant enters through the sliding door, shooting an annoyed glance to Sulsu as she pours another glass of jet. Sulsu watches the door as it closes, making fleeting eye contact with her s'chana keeper on the other side. She and Dant have grown tired of one another's bickering and unanimously decided to be silent to one another. At least for tonight. Dant points to the light above them. Sulsu rolls her eyes, but doesn't disagree. Dant waves his hand over the light sensor and the room goes dark. The two make their way under the blankets on their respective sides. Sulsu slides off her gown and curls herself into a ball, facing the wall. Dant arranges himself into a satisfactory position with austere blunt motions. Sulsu sighs. Perhaps they can find a normal rhythm in the tower soon enough. The issue with the islanders is over at least. Sulsu doubts that Kidra will any help to them. *Famed Oracle Pi Soulde.* Sulsu has seen her, always coming and going from Rhode's lab all night long. She has that child with her, who gets taller every time Sulsu sees her in the corridor.

45
Me
03/16/2500 6:56PM

And here I am. Being so young, I still cannot adequately relay my symptoms to the apathetic witnesses of my distress. I learned eventually that I am prone to migraines, but in the beginning, I had thought that the colorful images floating across my visual field were simply visions from the tunnels superimposed on the reality before me. These images appear sometimes benign, but more often than not, in the presence of another, an underlying machiavellianism creeps through. It is as if my own integrity is nothing against the two dimensional transparent representation of another's heart.

"Síofra," Elder Ish Tin says, approaching me with his usual reticence. He does not *dislike* me, rather he fears the antithetic nature of my being. Most of the others do.

"Yes?" I answer, tired of the silence. He looks concerned. I am growing quicker than expected. This I know by comparison. But, when I do speak, my voice is overly matured and results in an overall uncanny presentation.

"Well, I ... I thought you would like to attend tonight's conference with the oracles. We can go now if you wish." The elders seem to pay me more regard than they do my mother, or indeed the other dwellers of this tower, but Elder Ish Tin pays me particular attention. I nod and follow him slowly through the large hallway. I see no need to hurry my short legs and fall far behind. When he looks back at me, he jumps.

We enter the main hall. The elders and most oracles are already seated in large angular chairs. I had hoped, as I often hoped, that I would see my mother, but her chair is empty. But for our journeys to the caves, I find myself rarely in her company. Her preoccupation with the knowledge of the caves is leaving her ignorant to the world around her. Or perhaps just to me. In our moments together in the repetitiveness of time, I sometimes see her looking at me. Not in the strange way that the others do but in a sad way. She does not fear, but assumes, that I will dissolve into a myrlorx like her son Ghli. She is not alone in her concern. I see many futures in the caves and when I close my eyes, but my own is truly a mystery.

I sit on an empty chair, letting my feet dangle. Antrisse Le Tel is escorted into the hall and invited to stand before us. Her face is a mystery to me. There are times when I can see the secrets locked inside of others as easily here as if I were wandering in the caves, however now is not such a time.

"We would like to thank Isse for her bravery in our efforts against the Njuyutis. The oracles think this effort should not go unrewarded," Dolf says sheepishly. The status of the oracles has been shrinking. The once coveted role of scholars and advisors has mollified into that of sycophantic abettors.

"I give thanks to you on behalf of the elders," Elder Crih Yulah begins. "Indeed, it has given us cause to review your file. You have worked in multiple undercover projects over the years, have you not?"

Antrisse nods.

Crih smiles. "You are clearly a remarkable woman. I, for one, am most impressed. Based on your actions with the Njuyutis alone, you will need a reward."

Antrisse's face contorts itself into that of withered defeat. She looks down to the floor. I feel another migraine starting. The aura consumes my vision as the heart of Isse is revealed to me in small glances and wordless thoughts. She knows we are in danger.

"I'll get to the point, Isse," Elder Ish Tin says. "We see a future for you as an elder."

The oracles seated on the far end of the circle exchange subtle looks of disgust to one another. They had not anticipated Antrisse would be granted such a gift. I look back to Antrisse. Her eyes seem to be searching for something in my mother's empty chair. The agenda moves on to other more 'pressing' matters of the joint eldership. There had been concerns that the Cymtians would loath to travel across Tel Bridge following the incident with the Njuyutis, but this proved unfounded. High Elder Nwirin Nnion is expected to arrive soon with his auxiliaries to follow shortly. The virus sensors must remain off until the residue from the fire has been left for another month, lest we have a constant barrage of alarms until the lingering RNA from the fire dies off. This area is to remain inaccessible during the high elder's stay.

The pains within my head begin, pulsing with each heartbeat from my ribcage. The conversation goes on ad nauseum, each participant seeking little more than to prove their own intelligence. I fear they would go further in this pursuit would they say nothing at all. My focus falls to the window. The stained glass collects light seemingly from nowhere. Even the rudimentary shapes appear lovely in the glistening of colors. In the bottom corner, I see movement that gives me pause. There is a tall young man staring at me through the glass. His face is obscured by the specs of nothing invading my perception, but I know I have seen him before. Suddenly he is gone. My thoughts are interrupted by Elder Ish Tin. He concludes the meeting by volunteering to be Antrisse's mentor. He looks at me expectantly as we all rise from our chairs. Elder Ish Tin, Antrisse, and I walk through the main hall towards the stairwell to the lower level. They walk leisurely, allowing me to keep pace with ease.

"There are things you should know, Isse, before you decide to become an elder," Elder Ish Tin explains. "And I want you to clear your mind of any reservations beforehand."

"I have no reservations," she replies automatically.

"But you do," I say quietly. "You have thoughts, many questions, swirling through your mind."

Antrisse's eyes grow wide as she looks at me. Elder Ish Tin smiles, satisfied with my candor. "Don't be afraid now, girl," he says with a chuckle.

"I have no real reservations," she says, "For I know the elders always have a plan. But ..."

"Ah yes, what is it?"

"I worry about the joint eldership. What will stop the high elder of Cymt from plotting to seize total control?" Her gaze drops to the floor as we walk down the stairs.

"Nwirin ... he is but a shadow on the wall. A visible monster with us in the room, but of no matter to our destiny."

Antrisse looks back to Elder Ish Tin. I can see the fear behind the soft smile on her face. I see a flash of color again creeping its way across my eyes. She wants something. To change something. Her regret is tapered with desires to undo her lies. *Interesting.*

As we enter the laboratory, Elder Ish Tin becomes deliriously happy. He loves the idea of the machine almost as much as he loves himself. He begins tapping against the glowing open portal. Despite the fact the elders have thus far failed to utilize it properly, Elder Ish Tin is satisfied with the fact that my mother and I travel often.

"This is it, Isse," he says with a glee. "Soon enough all elders will be using this to gain knowledge. So far only little Síofra here and Kidra have had the luxury of seeing the true magnificence of what's inside."

Antrisse bites her lower lip.

"No doubt," he explains, "You have heard of the state that Kidra is in. The travels have made her flakier than ever, to say the least. But that will all be sorted soon enough.

More power. That's what the machine needs. More power, a bigger portal, easier transmute. And Síofra is fine with the travels, aren't you?"

"Yes," I reply. "I am fine with the travels." His logic falters often, but it is true that I suffer no motion sickness. I walk over to Nal in the corner of the room. She yawns, her wide jaw forcing out a powerful blow of hot air. I hope she won't mind our using her horn once more tonight. Nal is always brought here in the lower levels of the tower to rest once the elders have finished with her for the day. I let my cheek touch hers and then lead her to the machine. She touches her horn to the machine, accustomed to our journeys. As the glow of the machine increases, I ascend the ladder. I look at Antrisse, urging her to follow. She does, and we jump.

I feel relief as soon as I am in the caves. My headache is gone. I cannot see Antrisse in the darkness, but I know she is behind me. I reach out for her so she knows where I am and then move forward. I can usually lead myself towards a vague idea of what I want. Elder Ish Tin wishes for Isse to see the past, the early days of Great Sular. I look at the different streams, crawling forward with ease. I can sense Antrisse trailing behind, but her path remains accurate. I pause as I come to an opening to a large brightly lit room. *No.* The walls around me feel firm. I crawl a little bit further and feel again. Above, there is a small area that feels as if it will yield. Antrisse has caught up with me and I push her backwards as I gently pull a loose stone from its place. I crawl backwards as the rocks cascade down. Antrisse coughs loudly. I feel for the ceiling again and am satisfied that it is gone. I lead Antrisse upwards. We are in another room. *This will do.* I look at Antrisse again, appealing to her to brace herself. And then it takes us.

This memory is soft. I sense that Antrisse is here too, hidden within another watcher in the crowd. We are within a vast group of people, the majority of whom are looking towards an elaborate stage of three tall podiums in front, each hiding a stream of people in old fashioned suits. The green mock walls behind are a summons of the old world freedom that disappeared long ago. The colorful flags on either side of the stage wilt in the unnatural still in the air.

"We are continuing to work in close contact with military agencies," the first speaker states. He clears his throat. "May I stress that the advice for the general public following the outbreak *to stay at home* is no different than the advice that was issued following The Disaster nine days ago. The likelihood of further force majeure remains high." He looks back and forth around the stage before announcing the next speaker. "I leave it to chief medical microbiologist Trem Psy to take the floor."

I make my way through the crowd, trying to find the details of time that history so often misses. Standing out in the crowd of people is a young girl. She raises her lowered head only briefly to glance behind her, before tucking her chin down towards her clavicle. She has a rash on both cheeks that meet on the bridge of her nose.

Trem Psy taps on the two large microphones in front of him. His bright cheeks and friendly demeanor do nothing to distract from his obvious apprehension. He pushes papers from one side of the podium to the other, awkwardly trying to identify faces behind the bright lights. "As head of the affected virology lab," he tries to begin but stops to clear his throat. The girl lifts her head slightly.

"As you know," he tries again. "Following The Disaster and the first earthquake… That is, although the damage to local areas was small, the resulting damage to the reference laboratory had unprecedented consequences."

I feel a slight rumble beneath my feet. It is that of a very small earthquake, comparable to a microseism. From what I gather, there are many more significant yet to come. The people around me shift and begin to shout panicked whispers to one another.

Trem Psy continues, apparently not having noticed. "The confirmed symptoms of the infection result from an increased inflammatory response. The resulting long term effects of the increased cytokines that remain following the infection include impacted kidney function, altered hormone production, digestion irregularities, and inflammation to the skin. Whether or not this is transferred in DNA is unclear, but we feel that this cannot be ruled out at this present moment in time." As the frightened speculations within the crowd grow, the voice of Trem Psy becomes barely audible.

Another subtle vibration occurs and the crowd erupts into a frenzy. I feel myself being pushed to and fro as people clamor towards the exit. They push against one another angrily, in a desperate bid to punish *someone* for their fears. Within the chaos, I see the young girl. She remains still, by the stage, with tears filling her eyes.

I am pulled from the memory with a painful force. Antrisse appears distressed so I lead her to an exit from the tunnels of time. The force of my body against the floor is always the worst part of the travels. I stand and look down at my companion in time. Antrisse's eyes are wide. She cannot yet remember what we had seen. I explain to Elder Ish Tin the images of Trem Psy in the conference. He nods slowly. His face falls. A brief pulse of shame rushes through him. He does not want me to share his part in all of this to Antrisse. I see in him thoughts of the secret knowledge of the elders. The fear of the sickly people who became the myrlorx spread throughout Great Sular following The Disaster. Their treatment gradually worsened. Teven Ish Tin, in his youth, had been against the violent attitudes of the masses. It was only when he became an elder, in his forties, that he became disillusioned with the fight to protect the innocent. He became instrumental in the modern fabrication that myrlorx are inhuman things. I remain quiet on the matter. Elder Ish Tin excuses himself, absentmindedly. He disappears through the door and Antrisse rises, attempting to follow. She lingers in the doorway, looking back questioningly at me. I take advantage of her vulnerability, hoping to pierce through her mind more deeply. I reach for her hand and look into her eyes. Her thoughts of Hln are close to the surface. I see the realization she had when she watched him plummet to his death. The Njuyutis people had a larger plan that they did not share with her; They had purposely infected themselves before leaving with multiple strains of viruses from the islands. Hln had succeeded in exposing one individual from Great Sular. A virus of the islands is certainly likely to impact those of Great Sular with a great virulence. *Ah, the memory of the past really was fitting to her presence.* I often find the caves guide one back to one's present. It is the future that it steals. Antrisse's face goes pale and she breaks away from my grip.

46
Black
03/17/2500 5:01AM

Her eye continues to throb. Rhode looks into the dark reflection in the large screen and pulls her lower lid downwards. She steps back from the screen and retches. She gradually moves close again and inspects the hard black lump of her eyelid. The "black eye of the myrlorx", she remembers people saying when she was young. There were many tales in those days of the distorted shapes that the myrlorx body parts were destined to create. She backs onto

Sulsu's bed, placing her hand over her affected eye, as if she could hide the reality of the situation just as easily. Her mind whirls with the events of the last week. She still feels ashamed for not being able to save that man, though proud that she at least tried. She remembers running from the train of myrlorx all those months ago, leaving them to die as if she didn't care about their fates.

Now, she is running again. Sulsu has planned an escape for Rhode. As Rhode is presumed dead from the fire, no one will be looking for *her*. Rhode is to wait at the back entrance of the tower for Sulsu's s'chana keeper. She will be gone before sunrise. She just hopes he will arrive in a hauler big enough to bring Nal too. Sulsu has already persuaded Dant to busy himself in the main hall. *I'll wait a few minutes and then sneak out.* She feels her body rising to a stand, the impatience inside her overpowering her judgment. She forces her legs to move slowly as they make their way to the door. The doorway opens and Rhode looks at the emptiness of the corridor. The quietness is eerie. She moves in slow steps. The anticipation reminds her of when she embarked on the large transport ship to Cymt. She had seen one or two myrlorx staring vacantly as they floated away from Great Sular. She shudders. She pokes her head into her laboratory, expecting to find Nal waiting for her, but the room is empty but for the machine. The oscillating glow hits the edges of what used to be Rhode's scrap pile. The flickering shadows amplify the starkness of Nal's corner. *Where are you, Nal?* Rhode looks around the corridor, unsure of what to do. *Perhaps he has her ready outside.* Rhode opens the heavy door, which had been unlocked by Sulsu's s'chana keeper earlier this morning. She closes the door slowly behind her, terrified that any sound will give her away. She leans against the wall of the tower. Its pale surface appears blue against the predawn light. Soon, a small vehicle approaches. Rhode frowns at the size of it, but slowly walks closer. She cannot make out the face of the navigator. *This must be it.* A hand motions for her to hurry and she does. She walks over to the passenger side and an opening appears at the passenger side of the vehicle. She feels her body go rigid as she hears his voice.

"A little bird told me you needed a lift." It is the Cymt elder Nwirin Nnion. "Get in."

Rhode feels herself move into the vehicle, her body performing in perfect nauseating compliance with him just as it had in her time in Cymt. It is like her first memories in the caves, trapped in someone else's body as she experiences their life in a dissociated dream. She tries to speak but she cannot. The vehicle moves forward, speeding along on its pre-coordinated course. She can see his face from her peripheral vision. The elder looks distressed. As the vehicle accelerates, she hears him grumbling to himself.

After a few minutes, the vehicle wobbles. At first it is slight and then it becomes a violent rocking. Nwirin hits the navigation panel and the vehicle slows to a stop. Nwirin slaps his hand down against the panel. Rhode feels herself shaking. He exits the vehicle and circles it. "This country and their inferior materials! These elders run it with stupidity and cowardness!" He bangs on the passenger side, Rhode's gaze fixes forward. "Get out!" He shouts. "We'll go by foot." She turns her head to see him pointing to the bridge to Tel Bridge. He hits against the door, expectantly. To her horror, it begins to open in slow swirls. She feels his hand grip her arm. *Stop!* She feels the need to do something, like the caves, break free. Nwirin pulls hard on her arm, but she resists. Reaching for the panel, she turns the vehicle back on. The fuzzy screen is useless but the damaged control board triggers the release of the emergency tristick. Feeling herself slipping from the vehicle, she accelerates fast and the tightness to her arm is gone. She turns the vehicle around, nearly knocking herself off balance. The vehicle rocks as before, but she concentrates on moving forward.

As she passes the tower, getting further away from that bridge, she sees a mass of light. *A generator?* As she gets closer, she realizes it is a group of one hundred or so solceros. They are tied to a generator, with their horns forced into large electrical rotors. Rhode now understands the motivations behind all of the elders' talk of merging with Cymt. She slows the vehicle, racing out to search for Nal. Long troughs of jet are wedges tightly under the solceros' frightened faces. She notices that each of these solceros possesses a mild dark glow, like the jet itself. She looks around her again. The first hint of dawn sheds light on the empty field. She does not see anyone else, not even a s'chana keeper.

Rhode gets to work. She grabs hold of the rotors one by one and releases the solceros. Feeling multiple jolts of electricity, her hands begin to buzz, but thankfully the currents are dampened by the solceros' thick rubber-like skin. She comes upon a young solceros, whose horn appears almost larger than its body, reminding her of Nal when she was young. His body is limp under the rotor and cold. Rhode carries on, feeling the sadness pulse through her with the electricity. At last, they are free. The herd of surviving solceros look at Rhode and then run back towards the bridge. They move like a blur, faster than any machine. *Hurry across the bridge! Before they find you again.* To her surprise, they run directly into the sea. They swim through the waves with agility and poise towards the rising sun. *They will be safe for now at least.* When she turns around, she sees Nal.

"Oh, Nal!" She exclaims as she puts her arms around Nal's horn. "I didn't even recognise you!" Nal appears weakened and drowsy from the jet, but nudges against Rhode with the same enthusiasm as usual. Rhode urges her to run, "You'll be safe with them." But Nal remains by Rhode's side. Nal motions to her back. Rhode takes one more look behind her and then climbs onto Nal's back, holding her arms tightly around Nal's hump.

Nal races off quickly. Rhode is relieved to be traveling west again, but the journey is difficult. Solceros were not bred to be ridden and Rhode finds holding on is nearly impossible. Her blurred surroundings are nauseating and she can barely breath. At multiple points during the trek, Rhode regrets this means of travel. Eventually, Nal slows, much to Rhode's relief. The familiar small houses and cobblestone streets are empty this time. Fhi, the first city, is even more lackluster than during the Light Ceremony. She dismounts Nal with difficulty and lets herself drop hard onto the street. Side by side, they walk, while Rhode tries to decide on their next course of action. Whatever refuge Sulsu had planned for them must be compromised if *he* knew of their plan. *They know I'm alive.*

"Ligh' be t'ya!"

Rhode turns to see a woman standing outside the door of a three story house. *Mitya!* They were standing in front of Qriau Inn.

"Need a room, d'ya?" Mitya asks, smiling. Rhode searches for a look for recognition in her face, but cannot find one. Rhode pauses, chastising herself for forgetting the danger of being in this town. Now, she is face to face with Elder Ish Tin's daughter. "Ye' pet, huh?" Mitya points to Nal laughing. "Ther a quite popula' pets nowadays, aren'ay they? I've seen another wi' one too no' so long ago."

Rhode is puzzled. *She doesn't recognise me.* As her eyes look over the inn, she notices her reflection in the front window. She takes a step closer. The swelling is heavy on both of her eyes now, such that her appearance is drastically altered. As she begins to speak to Mitya, she notices her voice is deeply hoarse. Mitya is quite helpful and suggests a friend's empty barn that Rhode and Nal can stay in.

"It might not get along with t'dog, neither."

They make their way to the barn without incident. The barn is large. Though empty of livestock, insects crawl over the walls and the smell of bird waste sits solidly in the air. "You need to rest, Nal," Rhode whispers as Nal collapses down onto a pile of hay with a satisfied grunt. Rhode feels the swelling around her eyes, still uncertain of the cause. She sits down on the floor and removes her scroll, hoping to map out their journey further west. A news headline pops up over the map. Rhode presses the heading as soon as she sees Kidra's name. Kidra is standing with a large glass of jet in her hand. Her cheeks are gaunt and her eyes appear to be drooping. She is speaking in the tone of a public service announcement, seemingly encouraging the public to use jet for their own safety, without outright saying that jet will protect against any health ailments.

"And we all need our health now, more than ever. The elders and oracles of Great Sular and Cymt can confirm that a new virus is present in the eastern region of Great Sular," Kidra's trembling voice states. "We must all work together to prevent future infections."

Rhode looks down and sees the black necroses eating away at her arms and skin.

47
Siyalline
03/20/2500 6:16PM

I did not resist as they pierced the microchip into the skin at the back of my neck. Nor do I resist as they place the thin layer of siyalline over my skin. It binds me to restriction. Soon, the sharp needles are released from the siyalline skin into me. It is agony. My mother watches with her distracted gaze. She had made this choice for me to reap the benefits of a new skin, so I willingly obeyed. Elder Crih Yulah approaches me. No, he walks past me. He stands before the crowd and relays more half truths to the audience. I had not known the pain would last so long. The floating cameras hover around the crowd, ensuring to capture the special moment. This is the first ceremony with in-person viewers to occur since the myrlorx invasion. The people's faces are transfixed on me, some blank, some opened mouths. *And him*. I see him again. The tall man watching me from afar. And then he is gone. My mother nudges me with her arm and leads me off stage. Elder Ish Tin guides me to a chair. The prickling pain is easing but I dare not press my body against the chair. I look back at the audience.

"I hate them," I whisper. "Why do I hate them?"

My mother tuts her tongue and says in a quiet voice, "The blankness of fame creates a mirror to others. They shine all of their perceptions of goodness into it, you become their desires, their wishes, their longing. They love you so purely, it's an obsession. They want to know you, every last detail of you, eyes searching desperately to become intimately acquainted with your every perfect pore. And when they see a flicker of truth, the you behind the shining mirror, they feel attacked, lied to, coerced. Unless you show the cracks of yourself, strip yourself bare and march up to each individual you meet, you are doomed to be loathed. One way or another. Sooner or later. You *should* hate them, for they will hate you soon enough."

Elder Ish Tin looks concerningly at my mother. For her, time is falling away. She used to spend her time in the caves watching Ghli and listening to the growing hatred towards everything he was. Without the solceros horns, our travels have had to be paused. She wishes to go back soon. As do I. My destiny lies there. I can feel it.

"Perhaps you should retire for the night, Kidra," Elder Ish Tin offers. "Rest." My mother nods and walks away, without looking back at me. Elder Ish Tin turns to me. "You'll need to go back out there soon. Do you remember what you need to say?"

I nod. The pain has nearly subsided. He hands me the large glass of phosphorus jet and I take it back on stage. The crowd cheers quietly and I state my lines. I feel the wisdom of the caves is slowly being paved away by the mind numbingness of reality. The increased use of phosphorus jet has caused a measurable increase of nanosenic acid in the atmosphere. Elder Ish Tin has speculated that this will increase the energy potential of the machine. His fervor for the machine has only increased since the solceros disappeared. My part is complete and I remove myself happily from the cheering public's view. Following my performance, Ash La Kes stands before the crowd advertising another, 'distinct' type of phosphorus jet. The crowd is fixated on her. As she raises the glass to her lips, I see a black mark on her hand.

48
Dazed
04/09/2500 10:23AM

Sulsu sits alone on the floor of her room. A glass of jet lies broken on the floor next to her. The jet is rising into the air in a slow puff. She feels the claustrophobia of her surroundings all the more. When she orchestrated Rhode's escape, her expectation had been for Rhode to then help her escape from afar. Learning that her s'chana keeper had betrayed her is still like a knife to her heart. She looks at the door. There is nowhere she can go even if she were to find herself unescorted. She looks at the screen in front of her. The signs of a spreading disease are everywhere. On the screen, different people in different places can be seen with various sizes black lumps over their skin that expand almost perceptively. There have been few implications here and there of individuals dying from the disease. Sulsu suspects there are more. A growing unrest has developed among the people of Great Sular. There are rumors of protesters from the central regions making their way to the tower by foot, but this has yet to be confirmed.

"The sight of myrlorx is so disgustingly human,' Dant says, entering the room with full force and dimming the screen.

"They're not myrlorx. They're sick." Sulsu rolls her eyes and touches her finger to the floating jet. She brings it to her mouth.

"What's the difference?" Dant sighs and sits on the bed, his back against the headboard. "There's too many of them." He looks at Sulsu. "Doomed, I believe, is the appropriate word for the rest of us."

"Don' be dramatic, Dant." She brings the round jug of jet, from the side table, towards her and drinks it recklessly.

"Anyone left will be forced into an entirely different way of life."

"A way of life doesn't simply vanish. T' structure of a society will come full circle. Wha' leaves us will return when we least suspect it, anew, a' full force." Sulsu feels the pleasant effects of the jet's intoxication.

"And will destroy us again and again," Dant adds.

"And will destroy *you*," Sulsu laughs. "I hope anyway."

"You'll be gone before I will." Dant reaches forward to Sulsu and points to her bare shoulder. Sulsu turns her head, her vision blurred. She can see a small patch of black on her right shoulder. She yelps and tries to shake it off. The dry raised bumps on the black mark make the rest of her skin crawl. "The jet is not to blame for that, but no doubt it has weakened your immune system."

"What makes you such an expert?" Sulsu spits.

"Anyone can be if they just listen. This tower has given me ample time for that."

Sulsu looks upwards. "They knew?" Dant ignores her, sliding down into the bed. He closes his eyes. Sulsu frowns. He smells strongly of jet. Perhaps more than she. His vices may be baited in secret, but he is no better than the rest of them.

She looks back at the doorway and taps her foot. She opens the door and walks past her s'chana keeper. He follows her but retreats when she glares at him over her shoulder. She ascends the stairs of the tower, emboldened by the jet. She can hear many footsteps moving back and forth in the main hallway. As she reaches the top floor of the tower, the sounds become muted and strange and her vision has become warped. She tries to steady herself against the bannister, while looking at the many doors along the long elegantly designed hallway. Determined to find answers, she attempts to open a door. She presses her finger into the scanner and a red light flashes. The door remains closed. She moves on to another door, dragging her hand against the grooved wallpaper. Eventually, she finds success. This room is unlocked and is likely acting as a guest room. She stumbled inside the empty room. Waving her hands upwards, the lights and wall screen turn on.

She stumbles against the wall and then holds onto the surfaces around the room, searching for *something,* though she isn't sure what. Pulling open the doors of a dresser, one by one, she pushes clothes, books, and bottles aside, before she finds a scroll. She takes it and backs onto the room's bed. From the engravings, this is High Elder Nwirin Nnion's scroll. She opens it and reviews the files carefully. There seems to be little information. She opens a book within the scroll, only to find it is written entirely in Cymtian. The unusual words seem to float around the screen. She taps on it impatiently until the language changes. It appears to be an unfinished draft of a formal report. She starts reading.

The joint eldership had been completed under the unanimous advice of all Cymtian elders, save one. Since the dialogues began, evidence of the elders' of Great Sular ineffective rule has grown exponentially.

Sulsu slides through page after page until she finds what she is looking for.

The unfortunate virus spread to Cymt on 17/03/2500. The remaining researchers of Cymt confirm that this is the result of Great Sular's former conflict with the Njuyuti Islands. On 24/09/2499, the oracles of Great Sular constructed a bridge to aid in the travel between the countries. It is noteworthy that this was constructed without the explicit approval of the Cymtian Elders Council.

Sulsu's heart sinks as she reads on.

Due to the recklessness of such actions, the Cymtian Elders Council will advise war against Great Sular, ensuring our actions succeed in destroying the elders of Great Sular and those infected with the virus.

Before she can process the information, she hears footsteps in the hallway. She tries to keep herself still, but the room itself seems to be tilting. The footsteps stop and Sulsu stands to leave, still holding the scroll in her hand. She opens the door and stumbles to the hallway, reaching almost blindly in front of her. The blurring to her vision is increasing rapidly. She gasps in frustration as she reaches the bannister. Never had she been so eager to return to that little room.

49
Broken
04/09/2500 9:55PM

    The cool breeze of the night sneaks in the cracks of the tower, roaring in its quiet anger. There is a quiet in the air that is rarely present in the hastened movement of the duties of the day. Their evening meeting had concluded. Most of the elders and oracles retired to bed rather promptly. Now the emptiness reverberates off the walls over the two of them. Isse pulls her elder robes tightly around her in the dimly lit hall. The status that the robe had once represented to her now seems irrelevant within the mayhem of the world. The burden of politics has become nothing more than a fable. She wonders why humans are too often preoccupied with the extraneous gains of deception when the natural world is closing in on them by the second.

She approaches the silent Kidra. Kidra sits, still, on her chair in the otherwise empty main hall. Her padded gloves rub against the purple fabric. Isse had been told to treat Kidra delicately, that she knows more than most from her ventures in the tunnels. Isse has observed the change in Kidra. It is a stark difference when compared to their first meeting. The once confident and graceful woman is now a vacant shell, unable to see the people in front of her.

"Kidra?" She asks her. Kidra does not move. Isse moves closer to her. "*Kidra*," she repeats softly.

"When the shine turns to matte, you know it has taken hold." Kidra says, turning her neck slowly. Her eyes seem to focus on something else despite looking directly at Isse.

Isse feels herself backing away. "Please, Kidra. Maybe I can help you. You can tell me what you've seen in the caves."

"You do not care."

"I do. I want to know. Knowledge is useless if not utilized."

"And curiosity without compassion is just evil."

Isse considers this for a moment. "No, you're right." Isse turns around and walks to her chair in the great circle. She sits down. "It's their question, not mine. But I do wish you would speak to me, as an equal."

"If they want me to be the thing that they can blame, then let me. When it all crumbles, I won't have to cower to them anymore." Kidra's frame becomes full of motion and she lets her torso fall to lean against the armrest of her chair.

Kidra's voice hushes to a trembling whisper, "My daughter... is dying."

Isse is confused. "Síofra seems well, Kidra." *The Mystical Síofra.* How can it be that such a person, practically metaphysical in nature, can be vulnerable to the world?

Kidra shakes her head. "No. My Rhode." Kidra recounts to Isse her last journey to the caves. She witnessed the future as a farmer in Fhi. Entering a barn, she saw her. She forced herself through the body, his actions and voice. Rhode's body was swollen and blackened. Her skin dripped brown fluid which pooled beneath her. Nal lied next to her, deflated in her being. Kidra tried to comfort her. Even in her dazed state, Rhode recognised her and rejected her attempts.

"Get away from me," Rhode said through a swollen mouth.

"Rhode... why?"

"Why, because I hate you. You're everything that is purely evil in this world. You are static. Unmoved by truth, chiseled into antiquity of what you overheard to be moral in your stolen youth."

"You hate in me what you are yourself!" Kidra exclaims before stopping herself. "I am sorry, Rhode. I didn't know you were in such dangers."

"Of course you knew. Everything happened right there next to you. You knew, you pretended you didn't because you wanted to concentrate on other things, on the caves, on your oracleship, on anything else but what was right in front of you."

Kidra backed away. "That is not for me. That is not *for* people like us. That is some sick version of a distorted reality meant to cause intrigue and drama. To make someone else feel special. When we all know for certain that no one is special, whether singular or grouped. If you fall for that idea, you are not only weak but stupid. I thought more of you." She was pulled from the memory and she left the caves promptly. Rhode will die from the virus soon and there is nothing Kidra can do to intervene against the slow decay of Rhode's body. Suddenly, Kidra stands from her chair. "Leave me be, Isse!"

"Isse is only trying to help," Elder Ish Tin says, walking with long strides into the center of the hall.

Kidra looks away from him. "No," she mumbles. "I cannot talk anymore."

"You often seem to be unable to," Elder Ish Tin says, now standing in front of her. "Unless of course it involves Síofra. Or Rhode. Or something else irrelevant to you. What is this relentless curiosity for the shadows in time? It's pathetic. When you do nothing *with* it."

"I've been smelling things. Things that are not there. The smell of being enclosed within an indoor pool. But all that was years ago. And when I go to bed, I can smell the top of Ghli's head. His toddler head with little tufts of thin hair, deep within my pillow."

"You grow madder by the minute." He smirks, turning to Isse. "I have a task for you, Isse. Dant's wife was found unconscious in the tower, high floor, contagious likely.

Nwirin suggests they burn her, but I would like you to inspect what he left of the body."

Isse looks at him.

"As a dweller of the islands, perhaps you will have some insight on the nature of the virus."

Isse's eyes widen. *He knows. Síofra? And now he is dooming me to die of it as well.* Isse reluctantly agrees to inspect the body in the morning.

"Grand. Now, I have a task for you girls. Follow me." Elder Ish Tin leads them to the laboratory. The machine in the middle of the room has a glow that is only barely perceptible. "It won't work now. But give it time." Together, they lift the machine onto a levertay, allowing them to transfer it to the outside of the tower. They push it at Elder Ish Tin's instructions to the entrance of the bridge. When the task is complete, Elder Ish Tin stares admiringly at the machine. "I had been under the impression that Rhode had died in the fire, you know." His gaze does not move from the machine. "When I was informed by one of our own s'chana keepers that she was alive, I thought we were all doomed. A fate worse than a myrlorx." He turns to look at Kidra. Isse is frightened by his erratic expression. "But then I realized that time is no longer linear with the machine. There is no hope of safety in this world, but the caves are another matter. It may be a painful endeavor, but one we must undertake. A select few can start again." Kidra shakes her head frantically and motions to the machine. Elder Ish Tin thanks the exhausted Kidra for her efforts, ignoring Isse, and excuses himself. Without looking back, he says, "We must prepare for tomorrow, Kidra. The Cymtians have declared war. We have every hope of escaping into the tunnels before their first attack. Once the generators have restarted, time will be ours forever."

50
Gach Rud
04/10/2500 8:44AM

Kidra is uncertain of what to do. Her limbs are static and hard in the subordination that her life has become. The elders have positioned Síofra in front of the machine. Elder Ish Tin has removed wire after wire from the machine and is replacing it with longer strips of copper. Long silver wires are lined up, reaching far. Dolf hands Síofra a glass of jet with a thick straw, which she accepts, unguarded. Crih begins to peel the false skin from Síofra. She responds in muted whimpers. It must be agony for her, Kidra thinks. She stares into the swirling black of the jet, in the hopes that the pain will stop as the drink takes hold of her. Síofra's peeled skin is bright red. The marks of the new skin's injection have scabbed over and the oracle forces a strip of copper into one of them. Síofra stares at the morning sun, the brightness of spring, seemingly unaware of her predicament. The long copper strip is connected to the machine. Another silver strip is forced into Síofra's skin. It connects to the power generator in the distance. The machine begins to hum. The glow flickers as Síofra's eyes blink rapidly.

Kidra moans, feeling her body shake. The sense of fury over such a malfeasance melts her cold reluctance like the hot sun on a thin layer of frost. In a rapid series of movements, Kidra removes her dagger with her claw shaped glove and rushes towards Elder Ish Tin. He cries out in pain as she uses her body to thrust the knife into his chest. The others rush to his side, but Kidra is already at the silver strip, hacking away as sparks of electricity fly in all directions. The strip is cut in two and Síofra is broken from her daze. She collapses to the ground. S'chana keepers rush over from the tower's entrance in groups of one or two. Dant walks rapidly behind his guard, his anxious eyes eventually finding Kidra's.

As she kneels down next to a now conscious Síofra, plucking the copper strip from her skin, she waits for her arrest. When it doesn't come, she looks up and sees the s'chana keepers running past her towards the western part of the field. A group of Sularians, in the thousands, are traveling towards them in vehicles. It must be the protesters from the central regions. Rotelcopters can be heard in the distance as more s'chana keepers come to fight in the imminent battle. Dant appears in front of her and pulls her up by her robe. He points to Tel Bridge. An army of colossal rhee cyrbs, the ice vehicles of Cymt, are racing towards them. She looks at Dant.

"We're trapped," she whispers. She turns to the machine. Its glow is gone.

"We are more alike than I thought," He tells her, calmly. "We are simple beings trapped in an invisible box called circumstance." He walks around Kidra to the broken line of silver. "People are cruel. They speak of altruism and kindness, but the second you show any hint of vulnerability, of difference, they turn on you. Like a fawn in a pit of hungry wolves. It's tiresome to be around people. I'm tired. I'm nothing at the bottom and at the top I could still only *pretend* to be something. It was all an orchestrated farce from the elders, anyway, because anyone who gets near me can sense what I am. No better than a myrlorx. But maybe life is worthwhile to someone." He picks up the silver in one hand and the copper in the other, connecting the electricity with his body. The machine roars once again and a flash of green appears. Dant's body convulses violently on the ground, his grip hard around the wires.

The portal opening will be brief, as he lacks Síofra's power, but the jet in his body should be enough, heightened by the electrical current, to give them a few minutes. Kidra and Síofra climb the metal entranceway of the bridge. When they are high enough, Síofra leaps, disappearing into the portal with a single white flash. Kidra hesitates. She looks down at the oncoming crowd. The protesters, many of whom are marked by the virus, crash against the s'chana keepers. The s'chana keepers are soon overwhelmed as half of them are on the bridge, attempting to halt the Cymtians.

She watches as many fall into the ocean, leaving the rhee cyrbs unrestrained.

   A man is suddenly standing before the Cymtians, his arms outstretched. Kidra watches on and realizes he is just a hologram, the appearance of which looks like a younger version of Elder Teven Ish Tin. The hologram vanishes as it comes into contact with the vehicles. They screech to a stop and the soldiers disembark with smaller vehicles, continuing into Great Sular. As the glow of the portal begins to dim, Kidra resolves not to jump. *I don't want to know anymore,* she thinks. *Knowledge without the ability to act on it is just torture.* Dant's body is crushed by the oncoming protesters. They meet head on with the Cymtians just as they touch the entrance of the portal.

Epilogue
Now

The vehicles were crushed within the confining walls of the tunnels. Those who escaped tried to rush forward. But they kept coming one by one. The commotion, the fighting in the claustrophobic space was as expected. Once one person saw a flicker of light in the distance, they all grew desperate to get to it. Person after person, as they climbed from their vehicles, followed, each becoming more fearful than the next. Eventually, I found myself trapped beneath the stampede of people. Thrashing with fervor was useless. In time, I was able to pull myself away inch by inch. I remember looking back at the twisted bodies. Those who were not crushed, suffocated in the enclosed space. When the last of them perished, the bright shine of the surrounding walls dulled into a uniformed shade of gray.

I do not know how long ago that was. I crawled along for some time, always avoiding that turn off of death. Although I had broken away, freed myself from the blockade, I could feel them still. In the tunnels with me. Not just the physical pressure of my breath being forced away and my skin necrotising from their weight, but the immeasurable faction that they pushed in my direction. The joint judgment, meanness of the tunnels eventually quieted in the blackness. Then the loneliness began. Without being able to see and experience another, except for the intimacy of memories, was unearthly putrid. There was no escape from the memories of the world, the remnants of old sensation. And, still, there is no escape from my reality, the present moment throwing at me the harsh sensations of now, the future, the past. The past memories are as much a reality as the current moment in time. The harmony of such is soothing.

As I come to understand the essence of humans, I feel more one of them. Despite their actions, their each and every carefully planned decision, each choice resulted in consequences, both good and bad. Perhaps I can learn to appreciate the unfavorable residuum I find myself in. For its means came through an act of kindness.

At times, I think I can catch glimpses of a solceros roaming in the darkness. Here I shall wander, too, until what remains of my body is crushed by the tightness of the tunnels or the machine is burned by the expanding flames of the Sun. Humanity has been abolished by its own desire to hold the secrets of the universe. And now I, the last of us, am trapped in its own joint consciousness. I like to think that I can find the beauty in that.

Printed in Great Britain
by Amazon